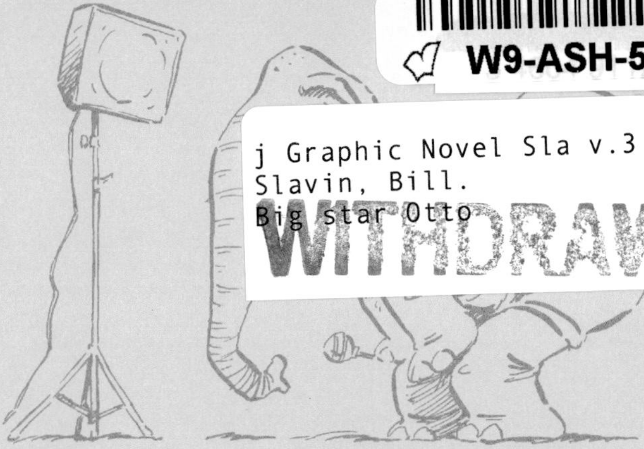

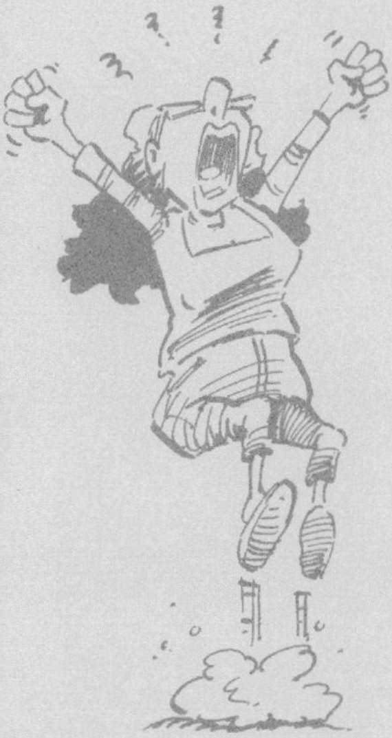

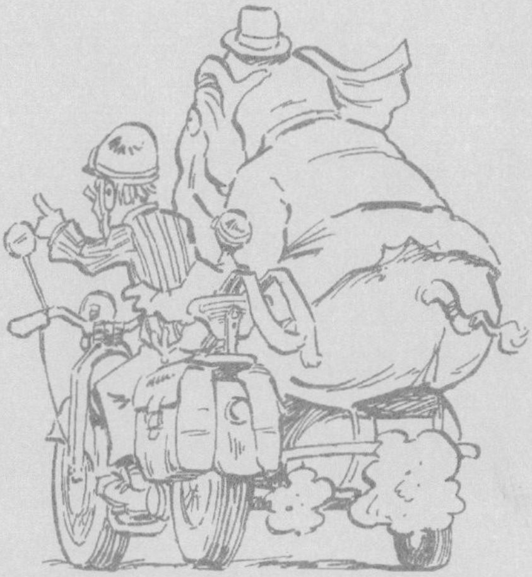

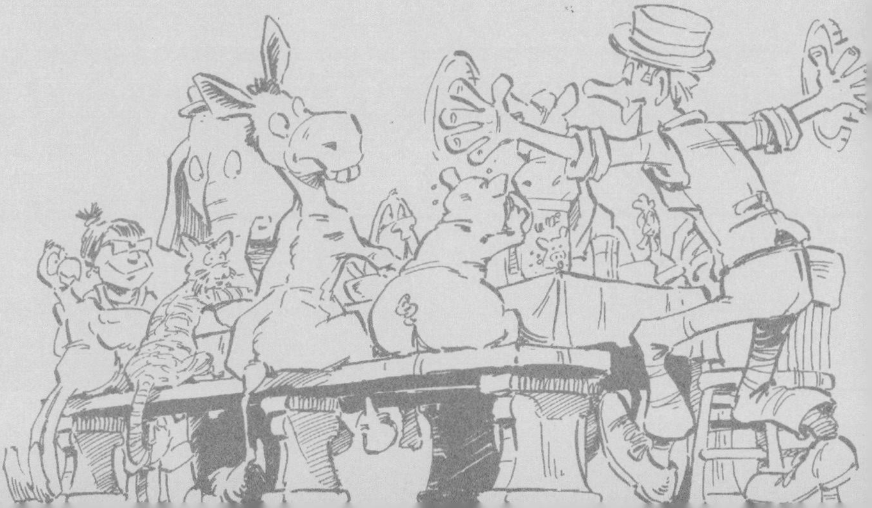

BIG STAR OTTO

WRITTEN BY BILL SLAVIN
WITH ESPERANÇA MELO
ART BY BILL SLAVIN

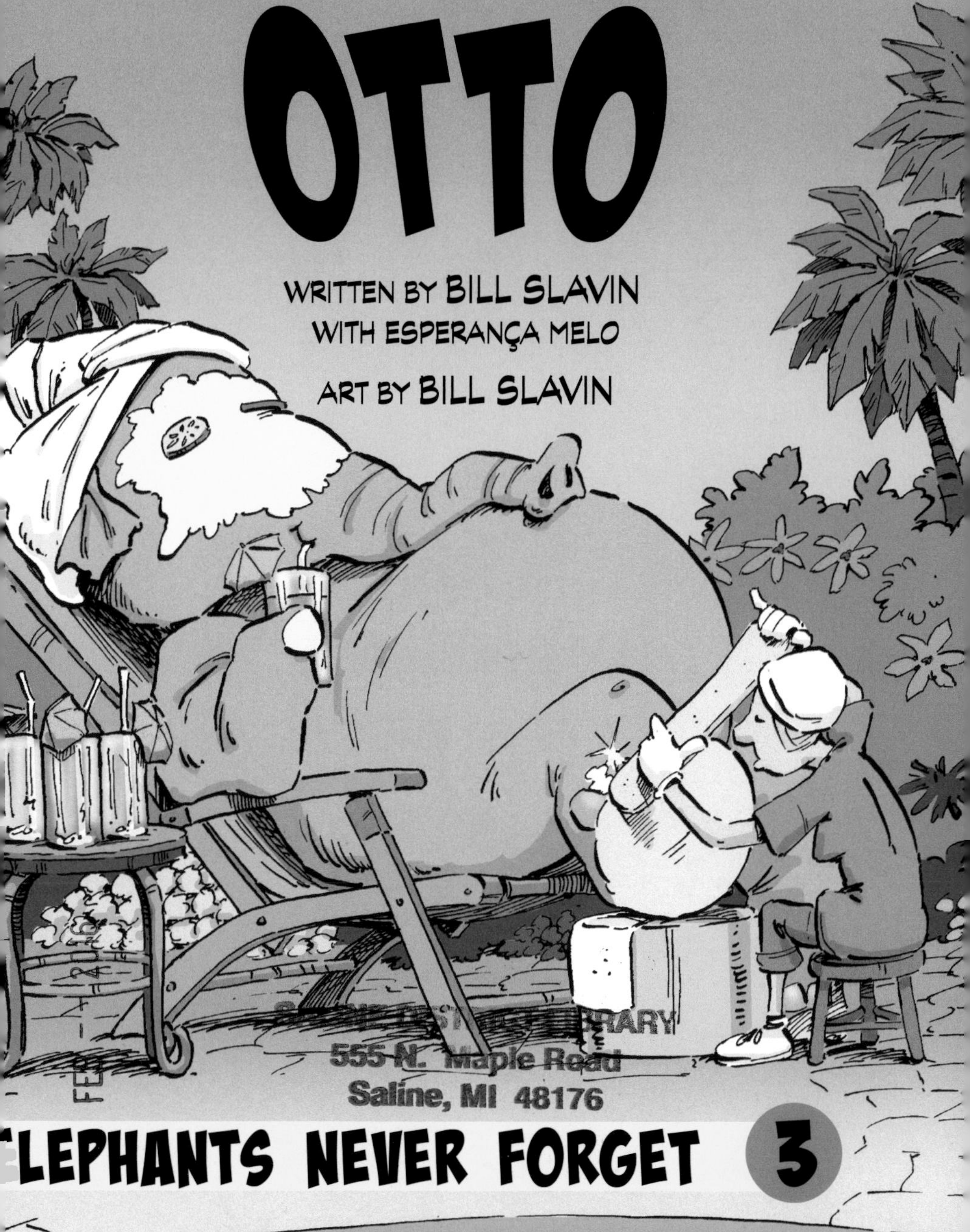

ELEPHANTS NEVER FORGET 3

KIDS CAN PRESS

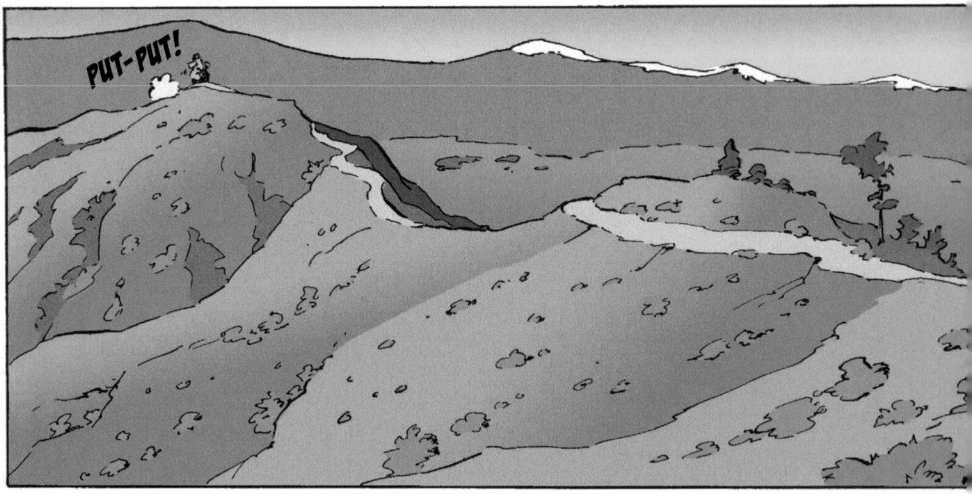
PUT-PUT!

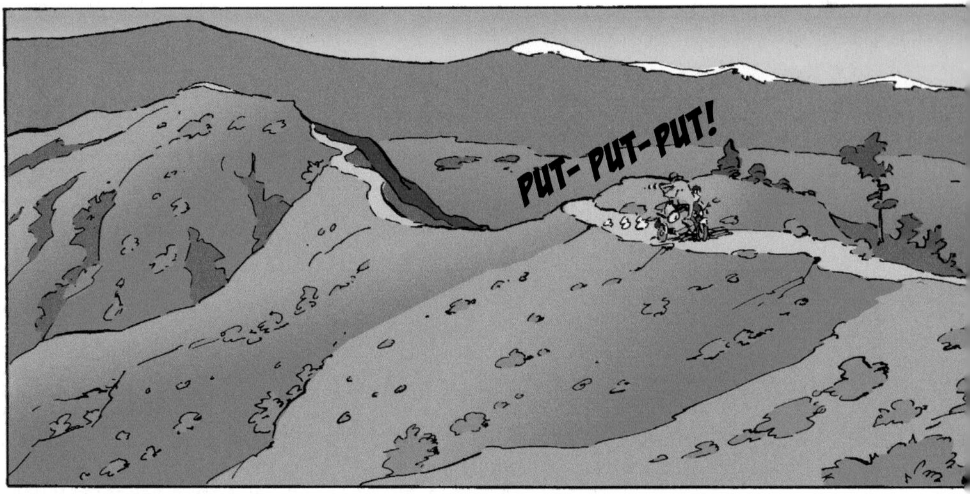
PUT- PUT-PUT!

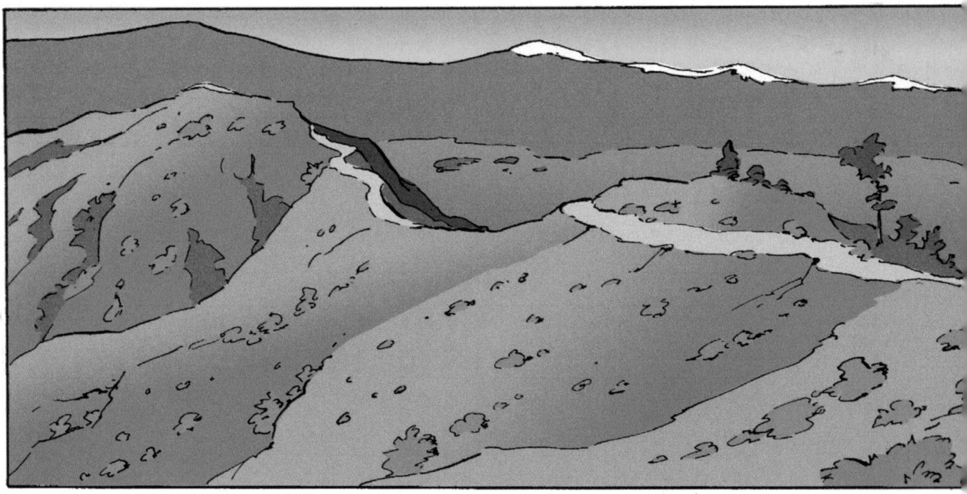

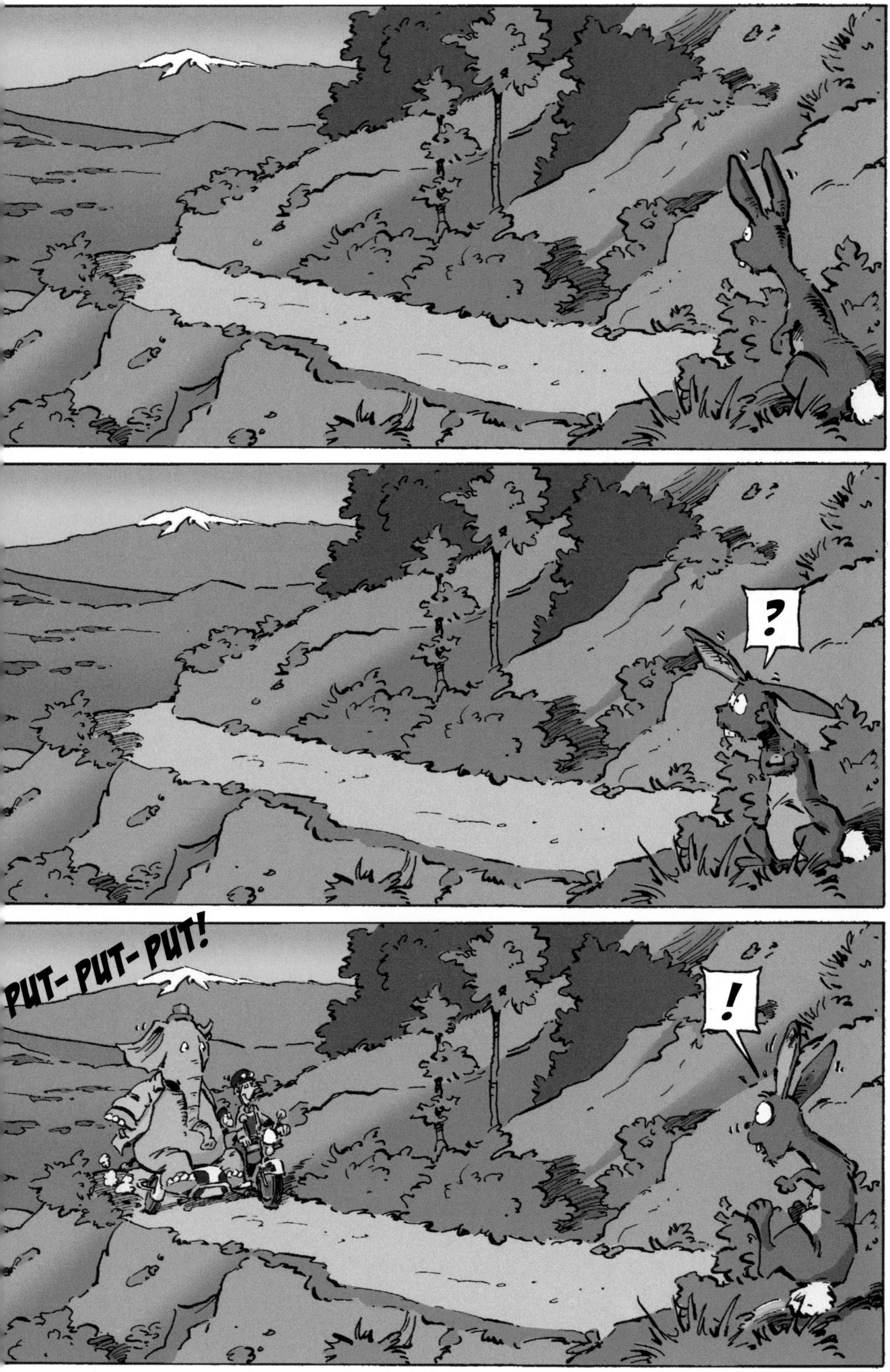
?
PUT- PUT- PUT!
!

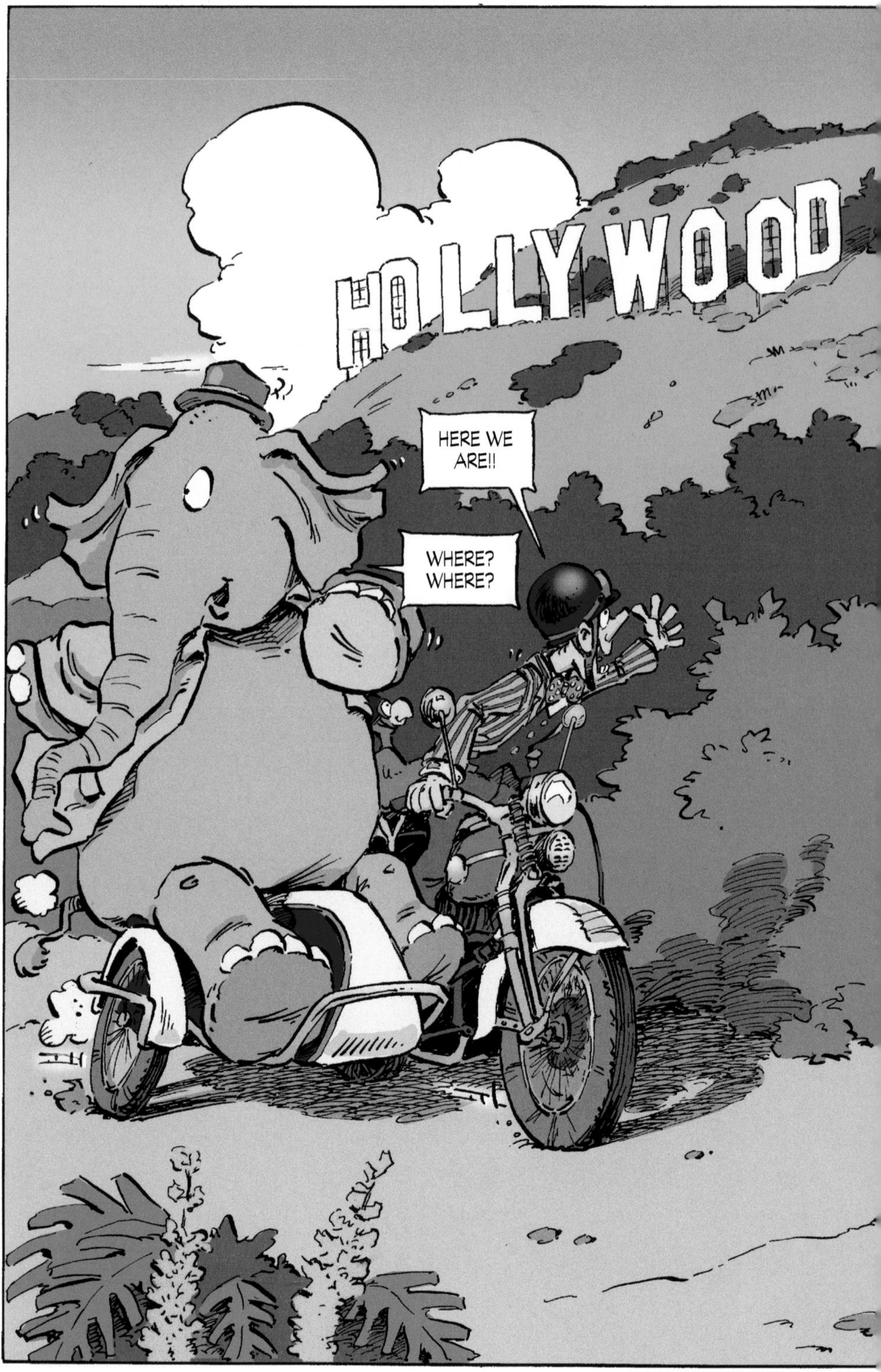
HOLLYWOOD
HERE WE ARE!!
WHERE? WHERE?

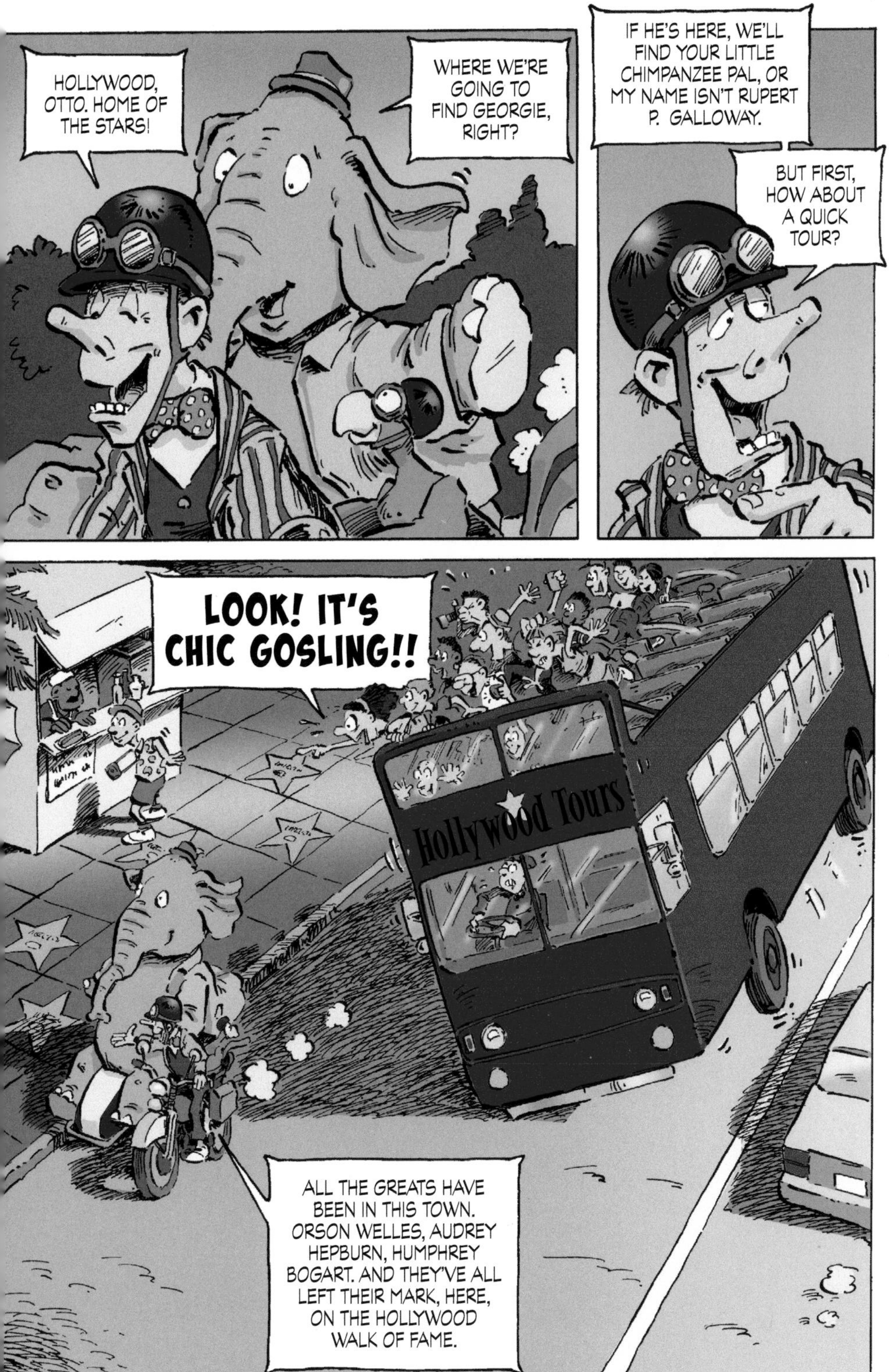
HOLLYWOOD, OTTO. HOME OF THE STARS!
WHERE WE'RE GOING TO FIND GEORGIE, RIGHT?
IF HE'S HERE, WE'LL FIND YOUR LITTLE CHIMPANZEE PAL, OR MY NAME ISN'T RUPERT P. GALLOWAY.
BUT FIRST, HOW ABOUT A QUICK TOUR?
LOOK! IT'S CHIC GOSLING!!
Hollywood Tours
ALL THE GREATS HAVE BEEN IN THIS TOWN. ORSON WELLES, AUDREY HEPBURN, HUMPHREY BOGART. AND THEY'VE ALL LEFT THEIR MARK, HERE, ON THE HOLLYWOOD WALK OF FAME.

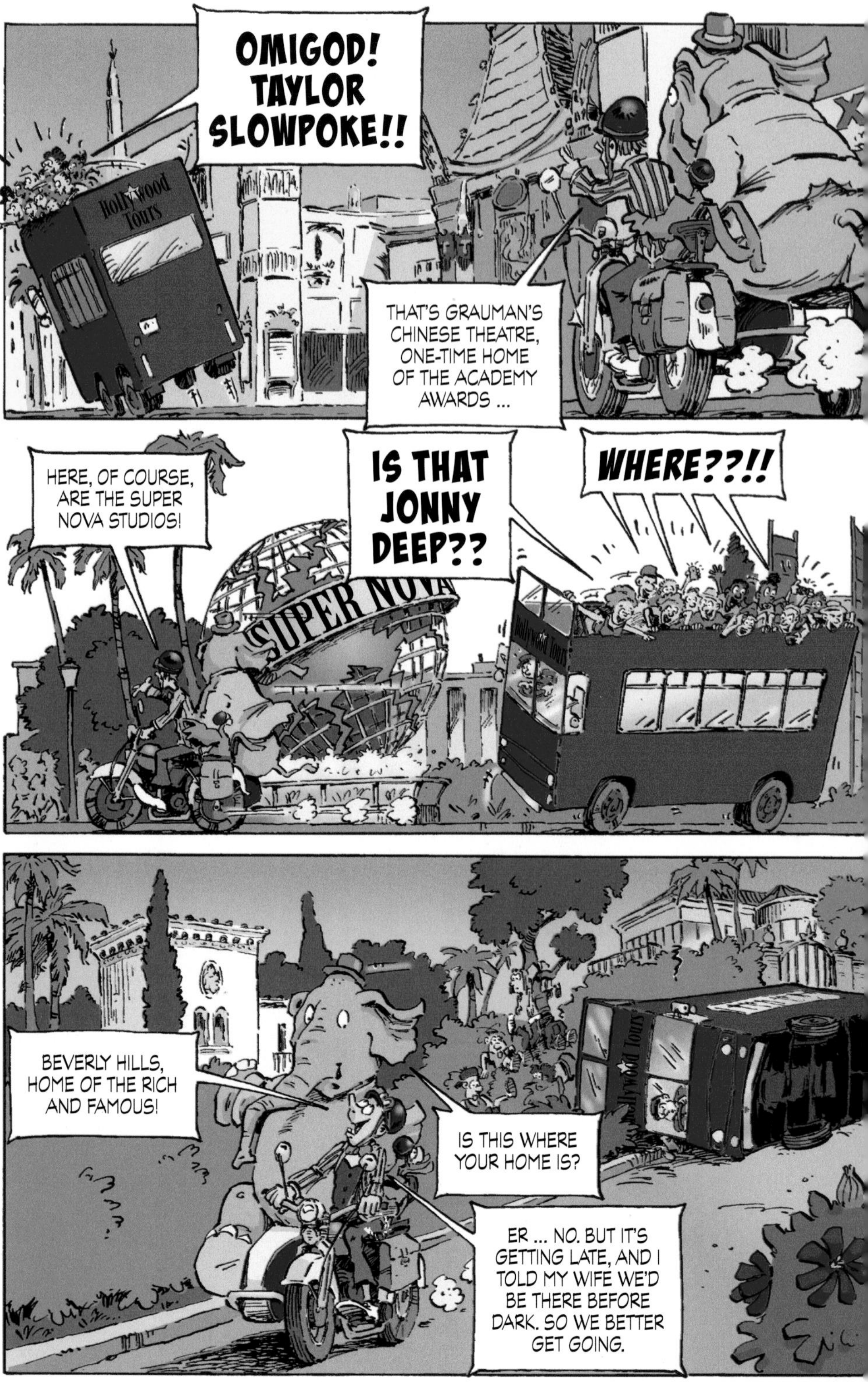
OMIGOD! TAYLOR SLOWPOKE!!
Hollywood Tours
THAT'S GRAUMAN'S CHINESE THEATRE, ONE-TIME HOME OF THE ACADEMY AWARDS ...
HERE, OF COURSE, ARE THE SUPER NOVA STUDIOS!
IS THAT JONNY DEEP??
WHERE??!!
SUPER NOVA
Hollywood Tours
BEVERLY HILLS, HOME OF THE RICH AND FAMOUS!
IS THIS WHERE YOUR HOME IS?
ER ... NO. BUT IT'S GETTING LATE, AND I TOLD MY WIFE WE'D BE THERE BEFORE DARK. SO WE BETTER GET GOING.

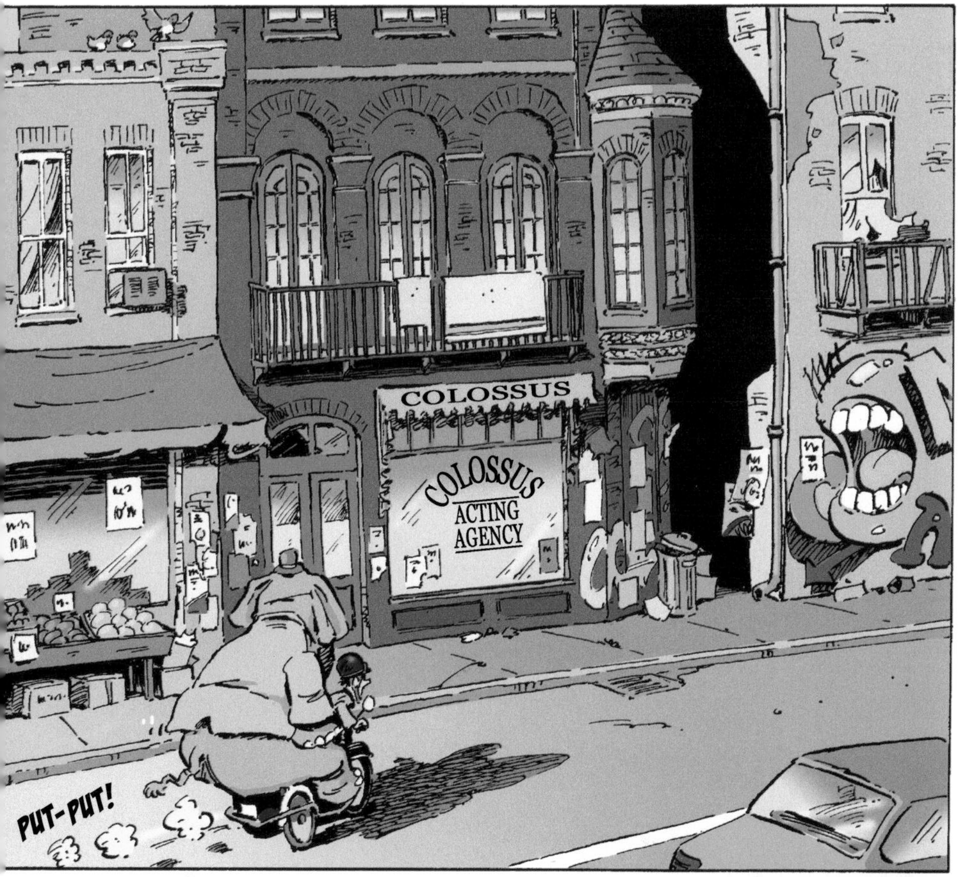
COLOSSUS
COLOSSUS
ACTING
AGENCY
PUT-PUT!

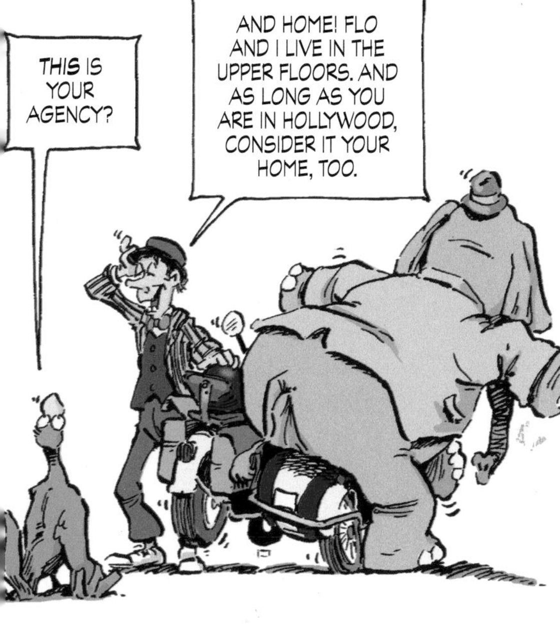
THIS IS YOUR AGENCY?
AND HOME! FLO AND I LIVE IN THE UPPER FLOORS. AND AS LONG AS YOU ARE IN HOLLYWOOD, CONSIDER IT YOUR HOME, TOO.

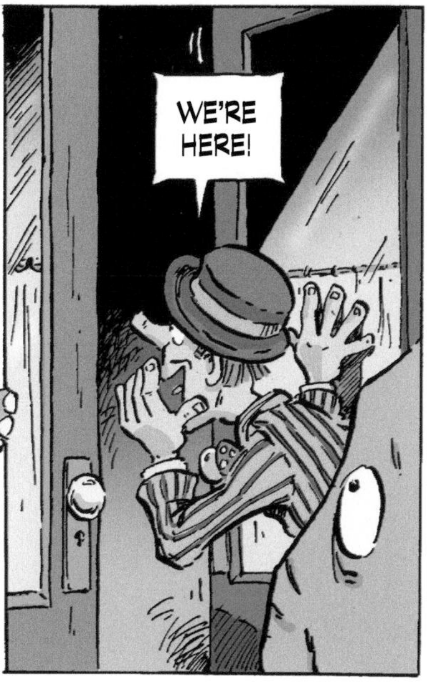
WE'RE HERE!

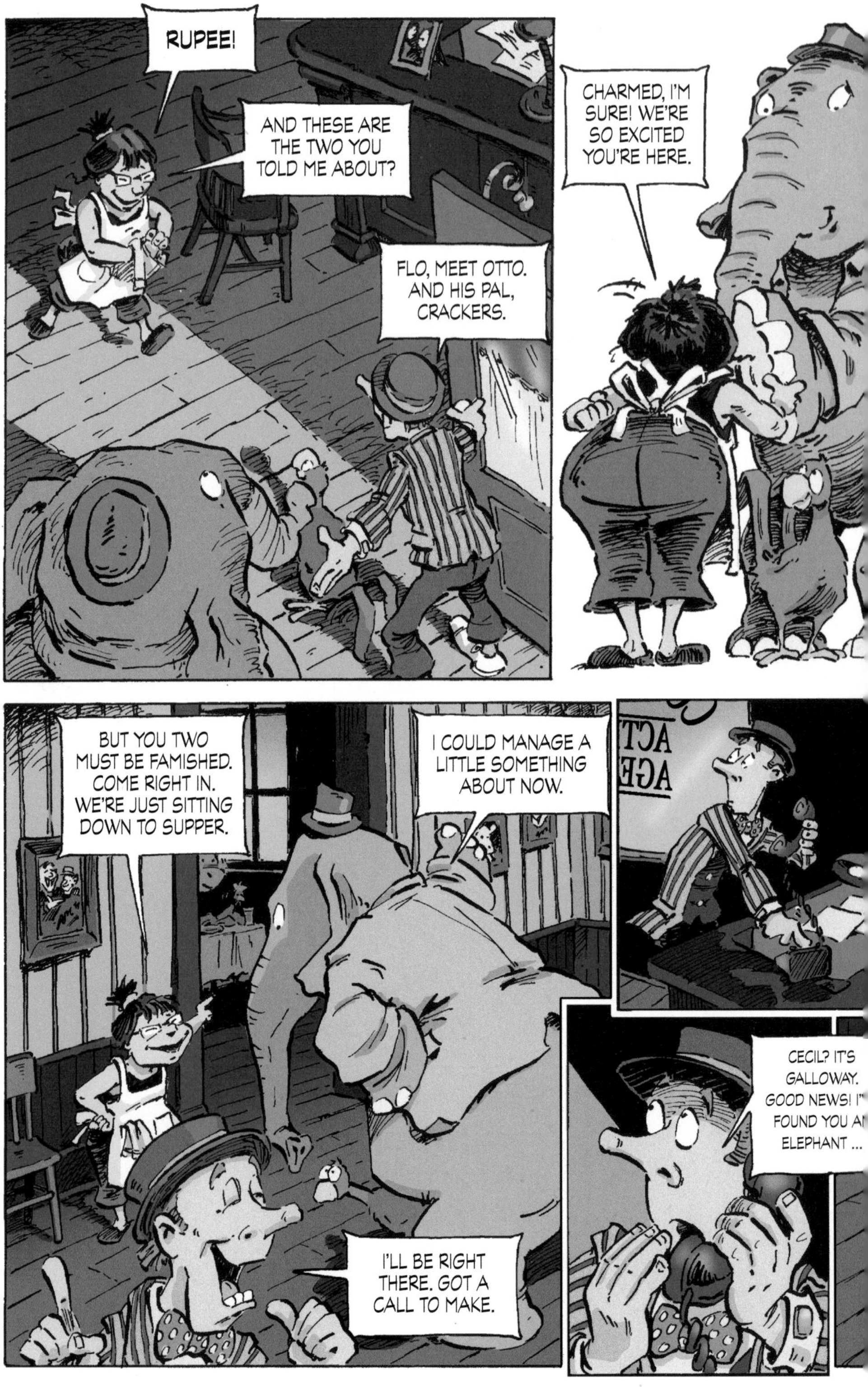
RUPEE!
AND THESE ARE THE TWO YOU TOLD ME ABOUT?
FLO, MEET OTTO. AND HIS PAL, CRACKERS.
CHARMED, I'M SURE! WE'RE SO EXCITED YOU'RE HERE.
BUT YOU TWO MUST BE FAMISHED. COME RIGHT IN. WE'RE JUST SITTING DOWN TO SUPPER.
I COULD MANAGE A LITTLE SOMETHING ABOUT NOW.
I'LL BE RIGHT THERE. GOT A CALL TO MAKE.
CECIL? IT'S GALLOWAY. GOOD NEWS! I' FOUND YOU A ELEPHANT ...

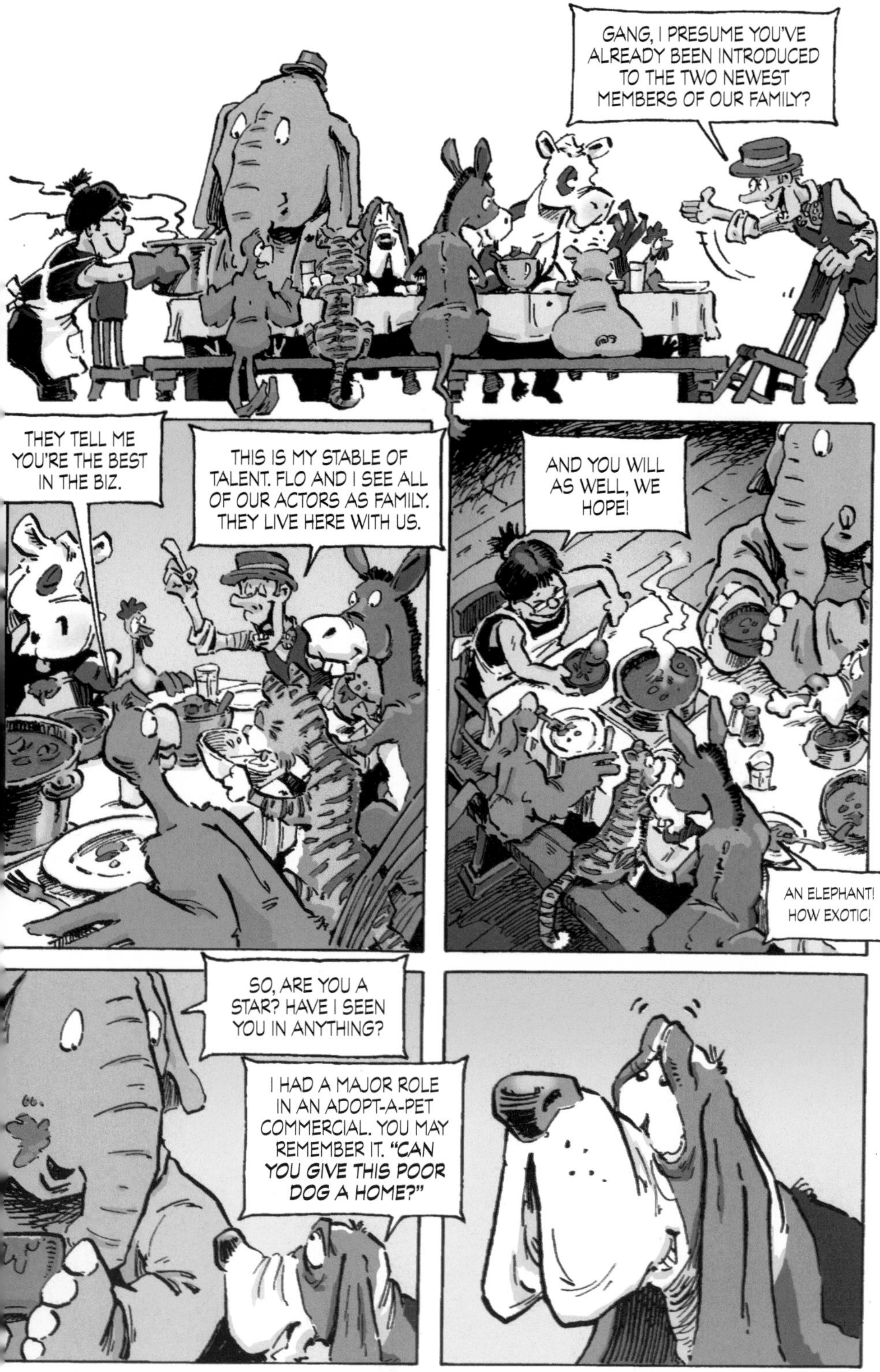
GANG, I PRESUME YOU'VE ALREADY BEEN INTRODUCED TO THE TWO NEWEST MEMBERS OF OUR FAMILY?
THEY TELL ME YOU'RE THE BEST IN THE BIZ.
THIS IS MY STABLE OF TALENT. FLO AND I SEE ALL OF OUR ACTORS AS FAMILY. THEY LIVE HERE WITH US.
AND YOU WILL AS WELL, WE HOPE!
AN ELEPHANT! HOW EXOTIC!
SO, ARE YOU A STAR? HAVE I SEEN YOU IN ANYTHING?
I HAD A MAJOR ROLE IN AN ADOPT-A-PET COMMERCIAL. YOU MAY REMEMBER IT. "CAN YOU GIVE THIS POOR DOG A HOME?"

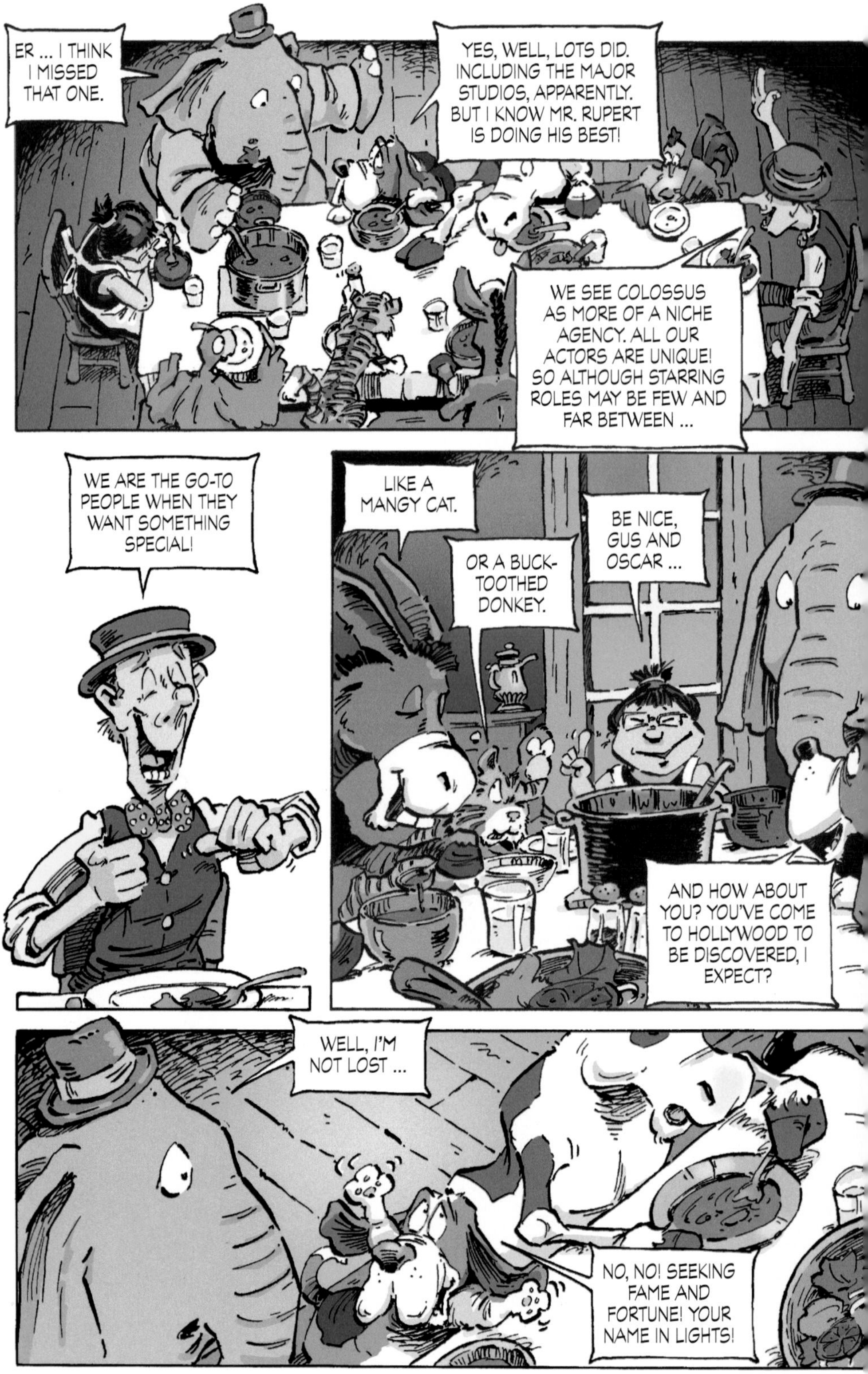
ER ... I THINK I MISSED THAT ONE.
YES, WELL, LOTS DID. INCLUDING THE MAJOR STUDIOS, APPARENTLY. BUT I KNOW MR. RUPERT IS DOING HIS BEST!
WE SEE COLOSSUS AS MORE OF A NICHE AGENCY. ALL OUR ACTORS ARE UNIQUE! SO ALTHOUGH STARRING ROLES MAY BE FEW AND FAR BETWEEN ...
WE ARE THE GO-TO PEOPLE WHEN THEY WANT SOMETHING SPECIAL!
LIKE A MANGY CAT.
OR A BUCK-TOOTHED DONKEY.
BE NICE, GUS AND OSCAR ...
AND HOW ABOUT YOU? YOU'VE COME TO HOLLYWOOD TO BE DISCOVERED, I EXPECT?
WELL, I'M NOT LOST ...
NO, NO! SEEKING FAME AND FORTUNE! YOUR NAME IN LIGHTS!

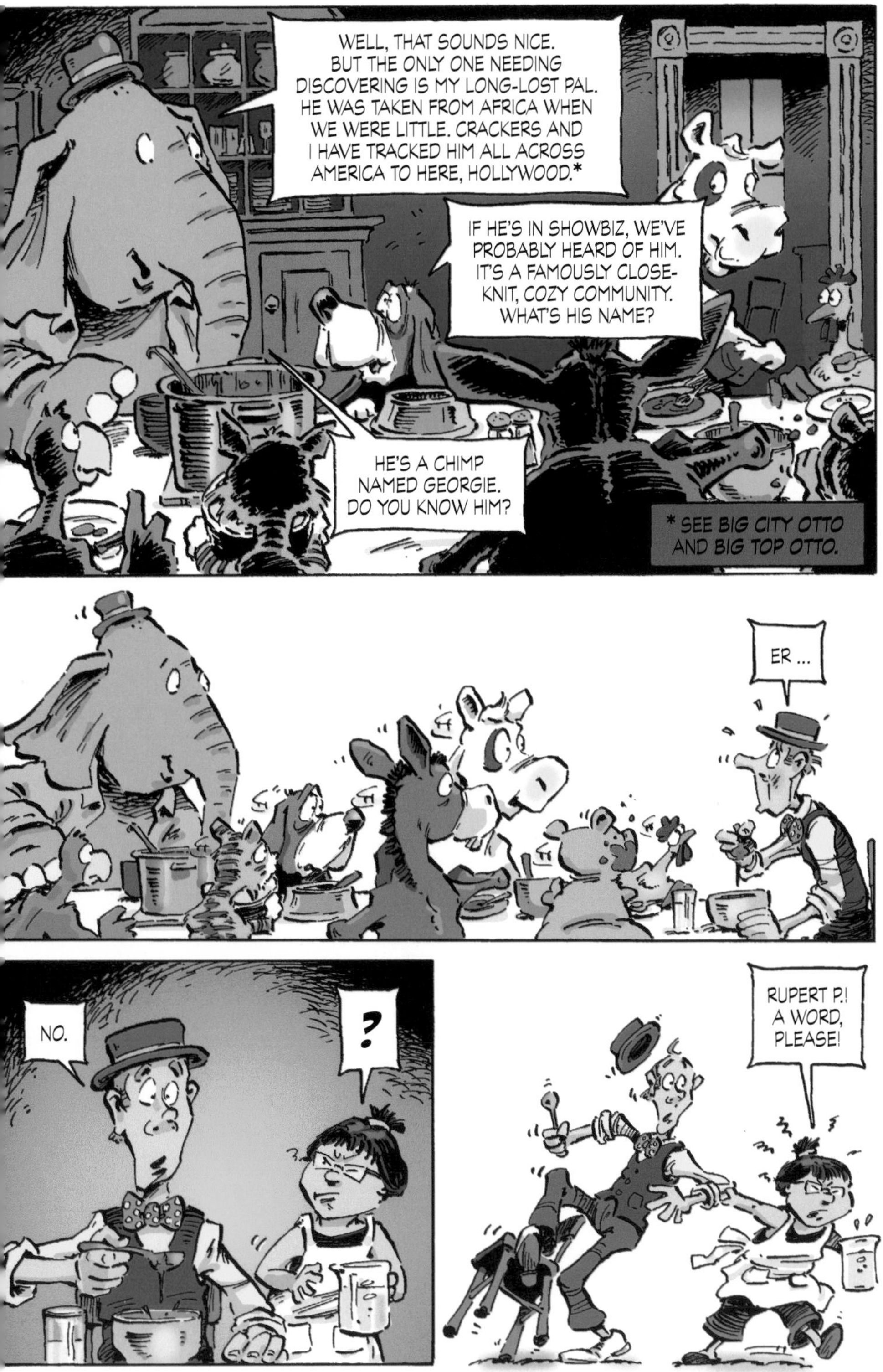
WELL, THAT SOUNDS NICE. BUT THE ONLY ONE NEEDING DISCOVERING IS MY LONG-LOST PAL. HE WAS TAKEN FROM AFRICA WHEN WE WERE LITTLE. CRACKERS AND I HAVE TRACKED HIM ALL ACROSS AMERICA TO HERE, HOLLYWOOD.*
IF HE'S IN SHOWBIZ, WE'VE PROBABLY HEARD OF HIM. IT'S A FAMOUSLY CLOSE-KNIT, COZY COMMUNITY. WHAT'S HIS NAME?
HE'S A CHIMP NAMED GEORGIE. DO YOU KNOW HIM?
* SEE BIG CITY OTTO AND BIG TOP OTTO.
ER ...
NO.
?
RUPERT P.! A WORD, PLEASE!

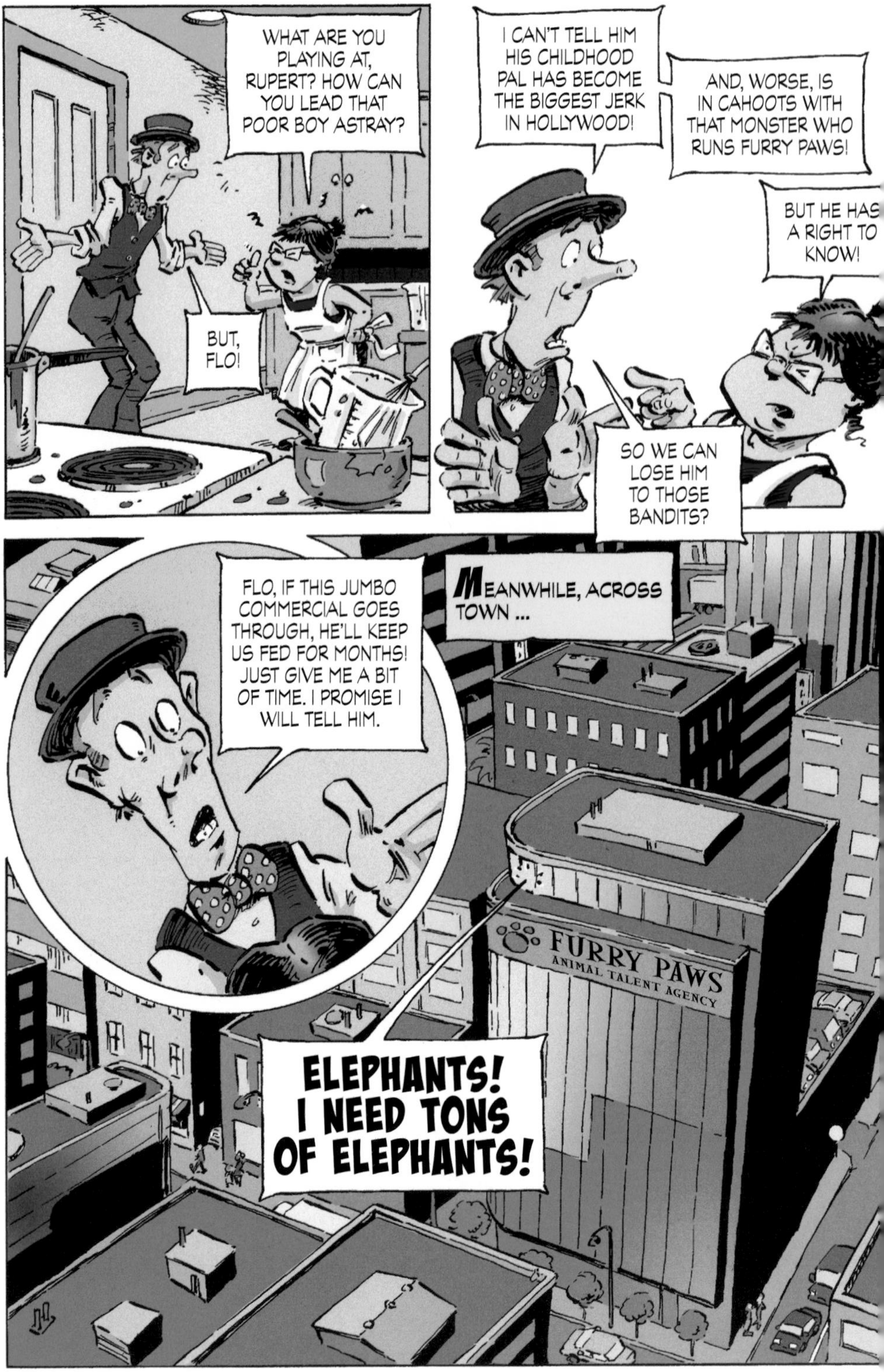
WHAT ARE YOU PLAYING AT, RUPERT? HOW CAN YOU LEAD THAT POOR BOY ASTRAY?
BUT, FLO!
I CAN'T TELL HIM HIS CHILDHOOD PAL HAS BECOME THE BIGGEST JERK IN HOLLYWOOD!
AND, WORSE, IS IN CAHOOTS WITH THAT MONSTER WHO RUNS FURRY PAWS!
BUT HE HAS A RIGHT TO KNOW!
SO WE CAN LOSE HIM TO THOSE BANDITS?
FLO, IF THIS JUMBO COMMERCIAL GOES THROUGH, HE'LL KEEP US FED FOR MONTHS! JUST GIVE ME A BIT OF TIME. I PROMISE I WILL TELL HIM.
MEANWHILE, ACROSS TOWN ...
FURRY PAWS
ANIMAL TALENT AGENCY
ELEPHANTS! I NEED TONS OF ELEPHANTS!

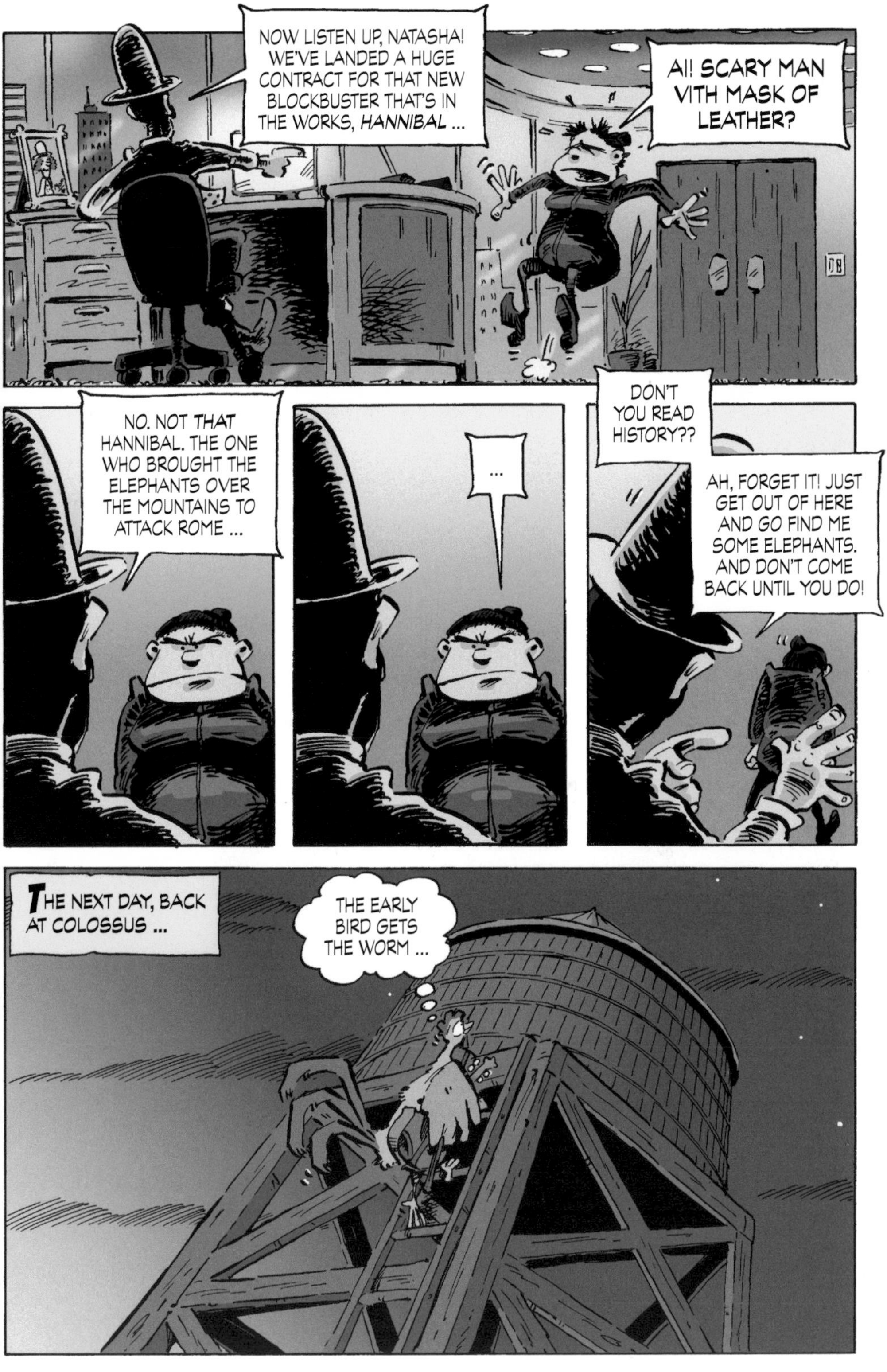
NOW LISTEN UP, NATASHA! WE'VE LANDED A HUGE CONTRACT FOR THAT NEW BLOCKBUSTER THAT'S IN THE WORKS, *HANNIBAL* ...
AI! SCARY MAN VITH MASK OF LEATHER?
NO. NOT *THAT* HANNIBAL. THE ONE WHO BROUGHT THE ELEPHANTS OVER THE MOUNTAINS TO ATTACK ROME ...
...
DON'T YOU READ HISTORY??
AH, FORGET IT! JUST GET OUT OF HERE AND GO FIND ME SOME ELEPHANTS. AND DON'T COME BACK UNTIL YOU DO!
THE NEXT DAY, BACK AT COLOSSUS ...
THE EARLY BIRD GETS THE WORM ...

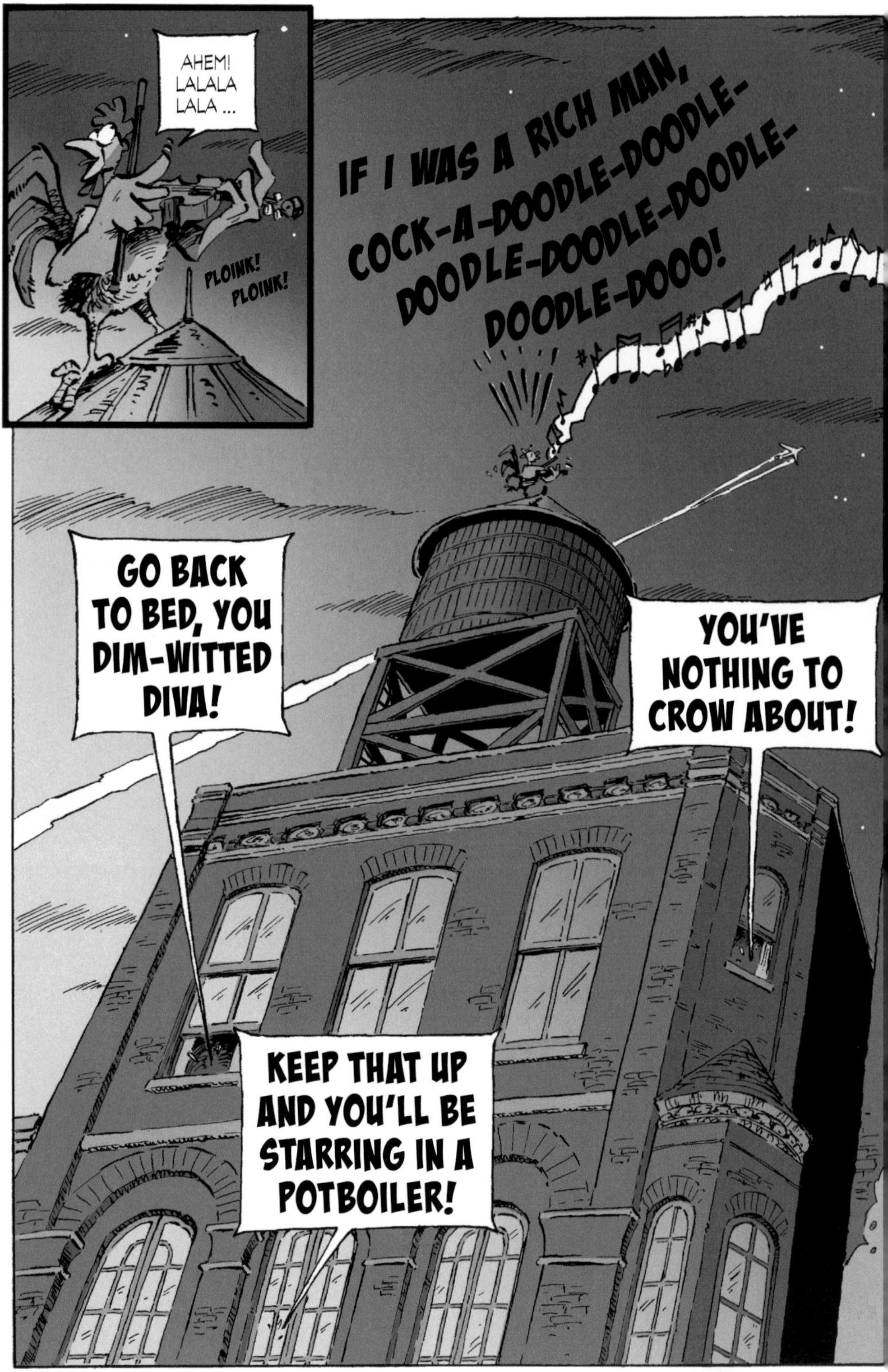
AHEM! LALALA LALA ...
PLOINK! PLOINK!
IF I WAS A RICH MAN, COCK-A-DOODLE-DOODLE-DOODLE-DOODLE-DOODLE-DOODLE-DOODLE-DOODLE-DOOO!
GO BACK TO BED, YOU DIM-WITTED DIVA!
YOU'VE NOTHING TO CROW ABOUT!
KEEP THAT UP AND YOU'LL BE STARRING IN A POTBOILER!

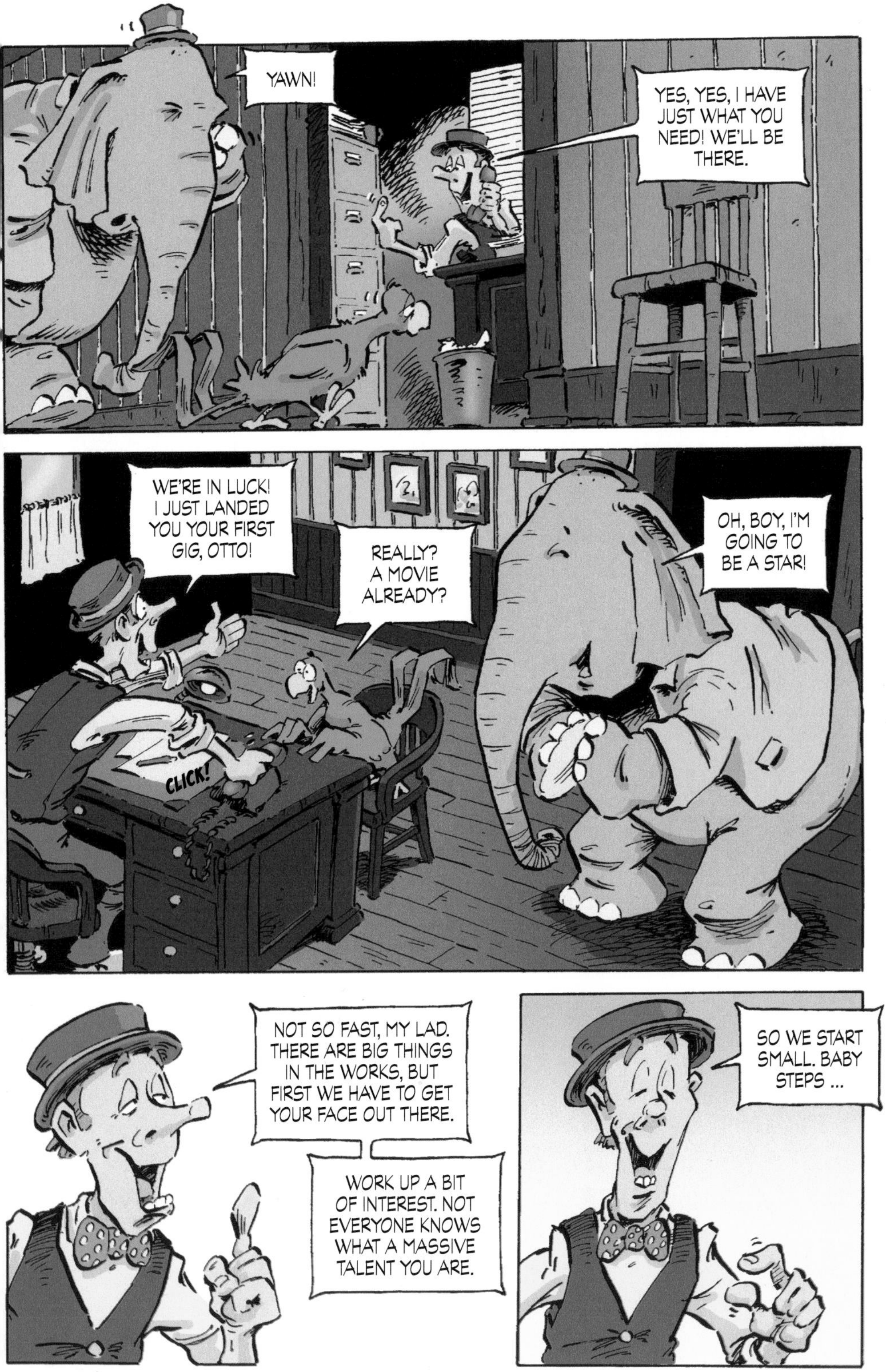
YAWN!
YES, YES, I HAVE JUST WHAT YOU NEED! WE'LL BE THERE.
WE'RE IN LUCK! I JUST LANDED YOU YOUR FIRST GIG, OTTO!
REALLY? A MOVIE ALREADY?
OH, BOY, I'M GOING TO BE A STAR!
CLICK!
NOT SO FAST, MY LAD. THERE ARE BIG THINGS IN THE WORKS, BUT FIRST WE HAVE TO GET YOUR FACE OUT THERE.
WORK UP A BIT OF INTEREST. NOT EVERYONE KNOWS WHAT A MASSIVE TALENT YOU ARE.
SO WE START SMALL. BABY STEPS ...

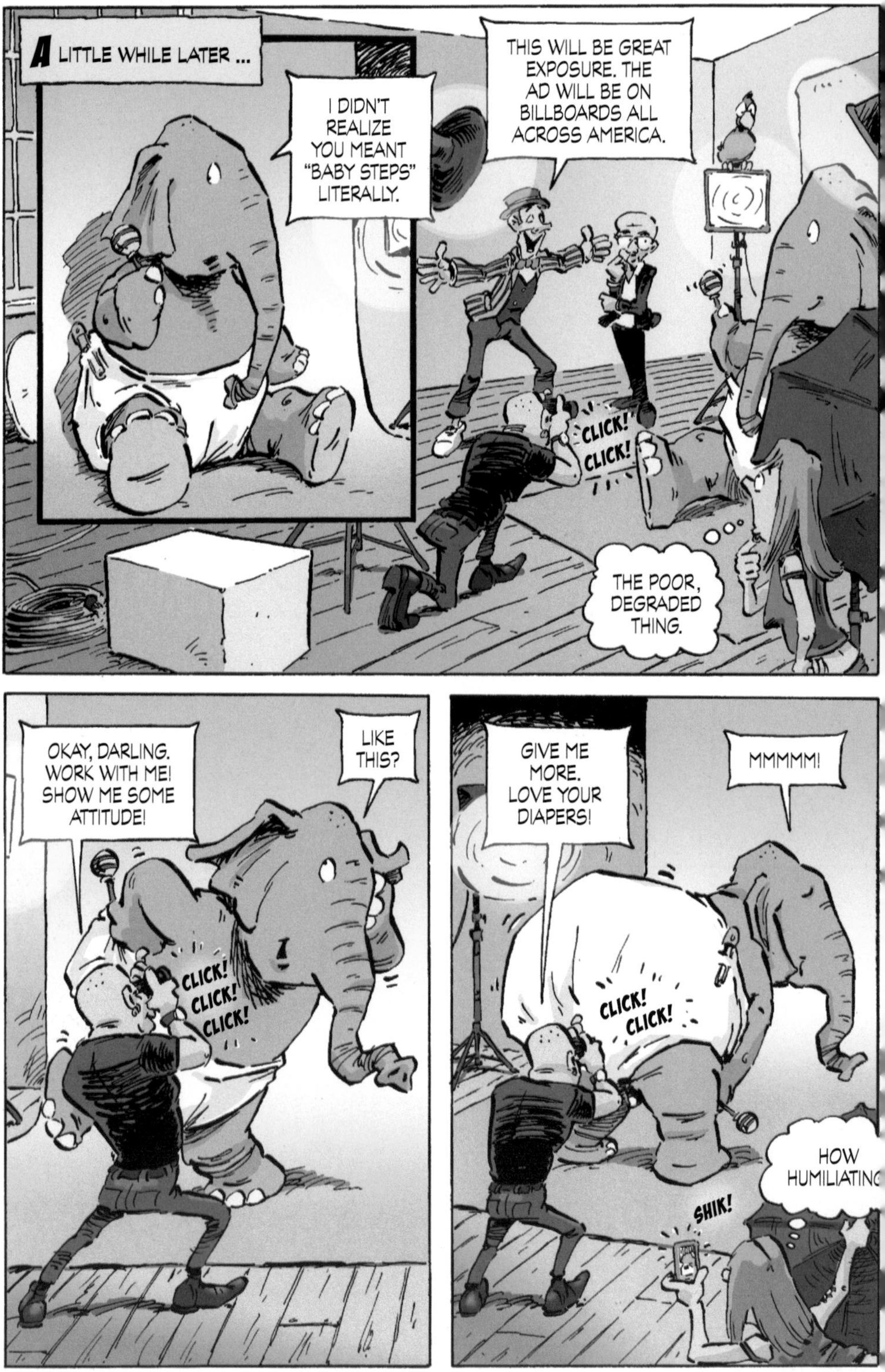
A LITTLE WHILE LATER ...
I DIDN'T REALIZE YOU MEANT "BABY STEPS" LITERALLY.
THIS WILL BE GREAT EXPOSURE. THE AD WILL BE ON BILLBOARDS ALL ACROSS AMERICA.
CLICK! CLICK!
THE POOR, DEGRADED THING.
OKAY, DARLING. WORK WITH ME! SHOW ME SOME ATTITUDE!
LIKE THIS?
CLICK! CLICK! CLICK!
GIVE ME MORE. LOVE YOUR DIAPERS!
MMMMM!
CLICK! CLICK!
HOW HUMILIATING
SHIK!

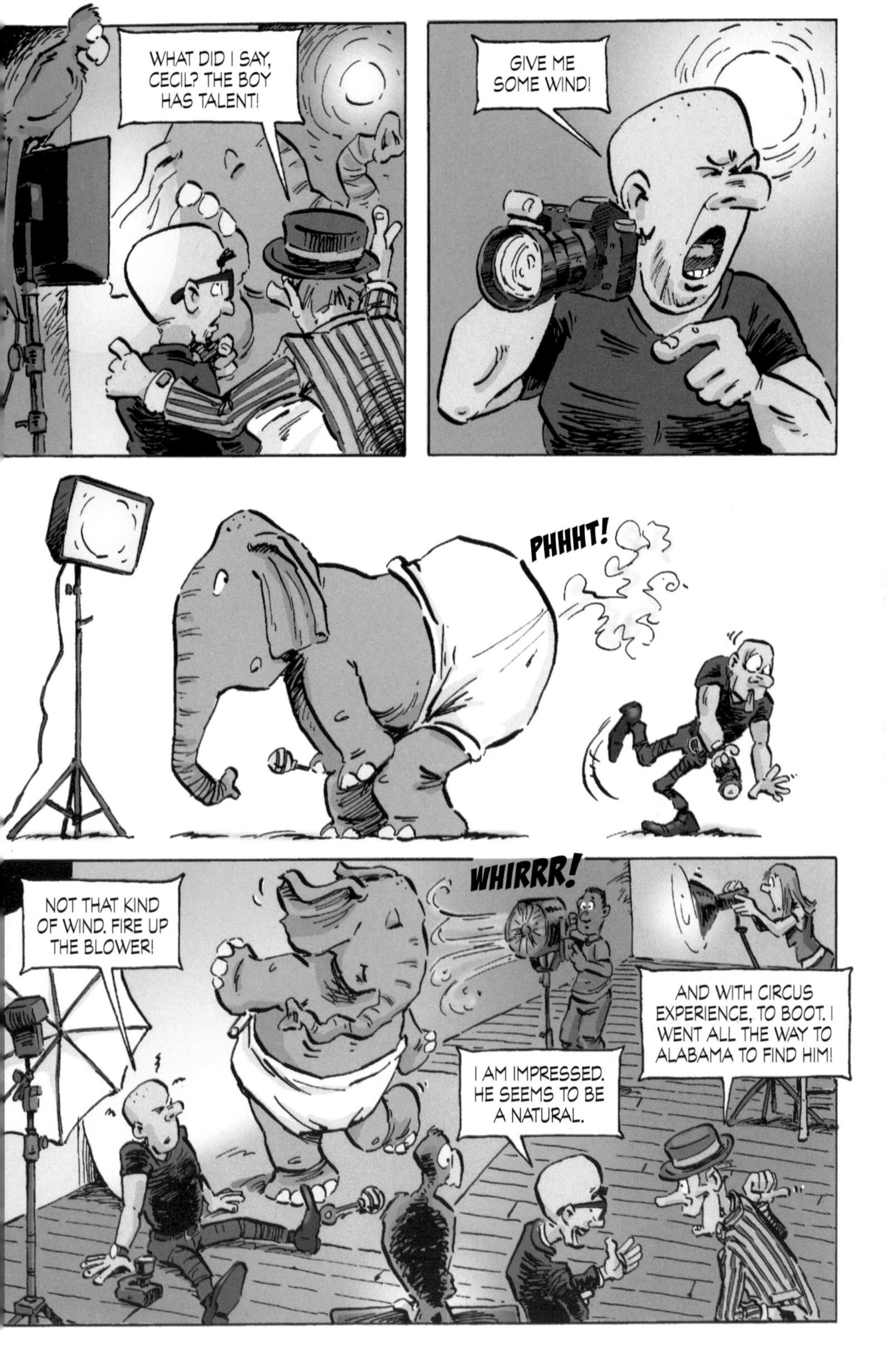
WHAT DID I SAY, CECIL? THE BOY HAS TALENT!
GIVE ME SOME WIND!
PHHHT!
WHIRRR!
NOT THAT KIND OF WIND. FIRE UP THE BLOWER!
AND WITH CIRCUS EXPERIENCE, TO BOOT. I WENT ALL THE WAY TO ALABAMA TO FIND HIM!
I AM IMPRESSED. HE SEEMS TO BE A NATURAL.

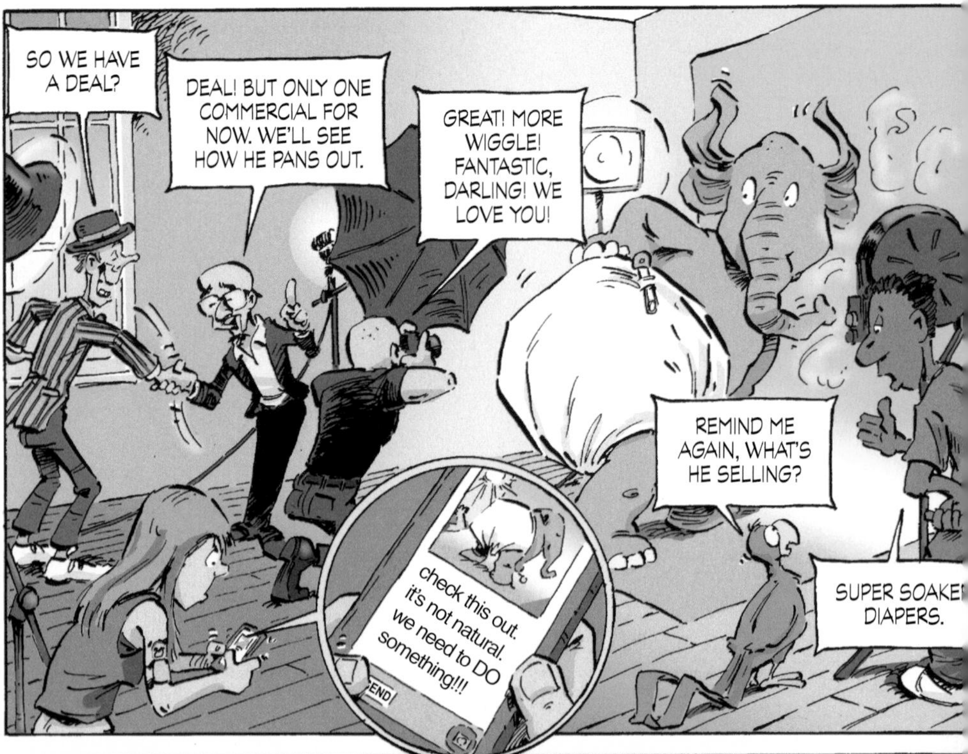
SO WE HAVE A DEAL?
DEAL! BUT ONLY ONE COMMERCIAL FOR NOW. WE'LL SEE HOW HE PANS OUT.
GREAT! MORE WIGGLE! FANTASTIC, DARLING! WE LOVE YOU!
check this out. it's not natural. we need to DO something!!!
END
REMIND ME AGAIN, WHAT'S HE SELLING?
SUPER SOAKE
DIAPERS.

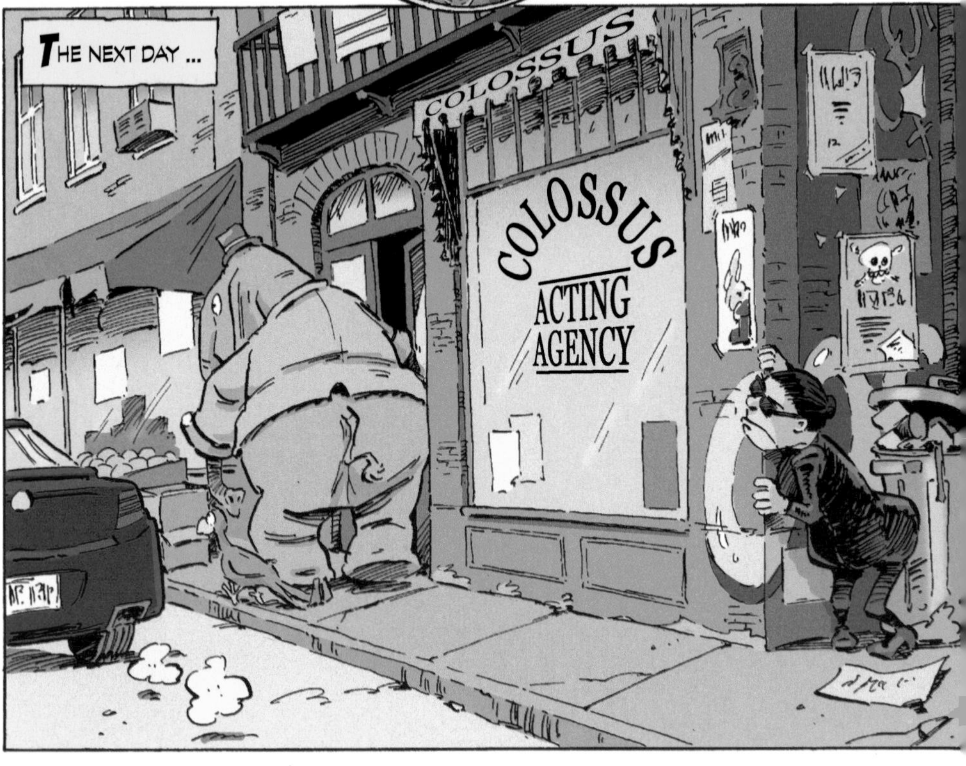
THE NEXT DAY ...
COLOSSUS
COLOSSUS
COLOSSUS
ACTING AGENCY

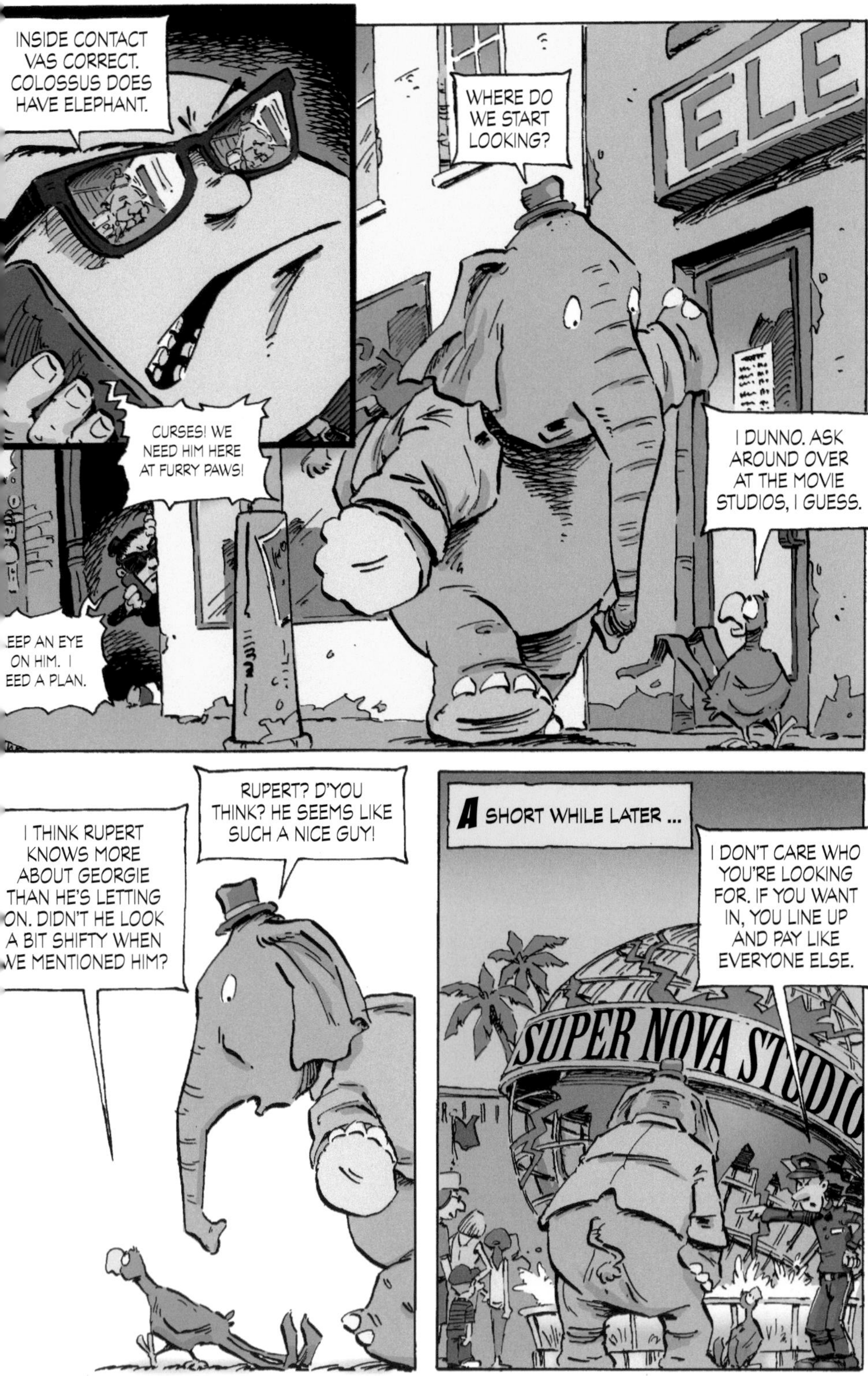
INSIDE CONTACT VAS CORRECT. COLOSSUS DOES HAVE ELEPHANT.
CURSES! WE NEED HIM HERE AT FURRY PAWS!
EEP AN EYE ON HIM. I EED A PLAN.
WHERE DO WE START LOOKING?
I DUNNO. ASK AROUND OVER AT THE MOVIE STUDIOS, I GUESS.
ELE
I THINK RUPERT KNOWS MORE ABOUT GEORGIE THAN HE'S LETTING ON. DIDN'T HE LOOK A BIT SHIFTY WHEN VE MENTIONED HIM?
RUPERT? D'YOU THINK? HE SEEMS LIKE SUCH A NICE GUY!
A SHORT WHILE LATER ...
I DON'T CARE WHO YOU'RE LOOKING FOR. IF YOU WANT IN, YOU LINE UP AND PAY LIKE EVERYONE ELSE.
SUPER NOVA STUDIO

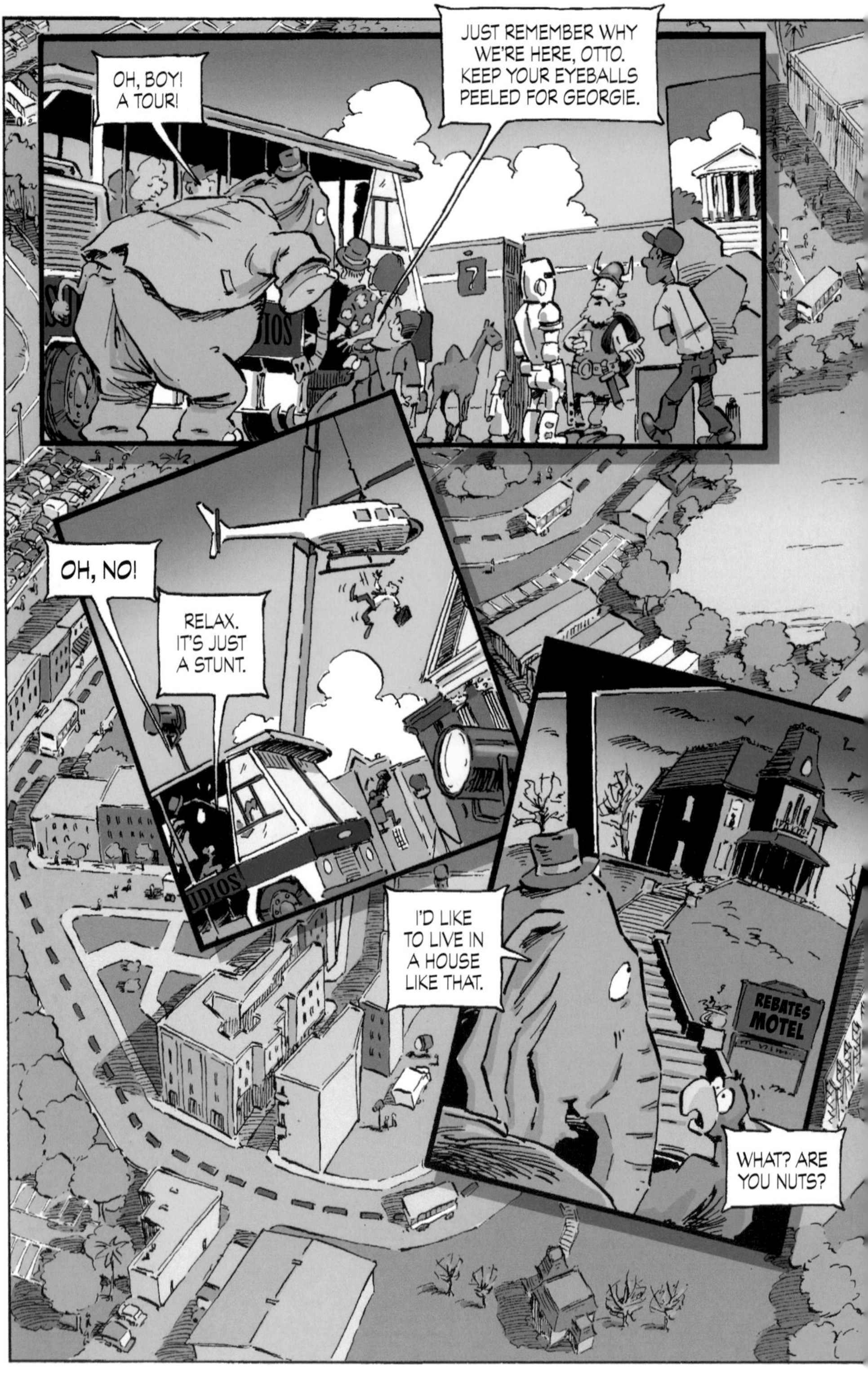
OH, BOY! A TOUR!
JUST REMEMBER WHY WE'RE HERE, OTTO. KEEP YOUR EYEBALLS PEELED FOR GEORGIE.
7
OH, NO!
RELAX. IT'S JUST A STUNT.
I'D LIKE TO LIVE IN A HOUSE LIKE THAT.
REBATES MOTEL
WHAT? ARE YOU NUTS?

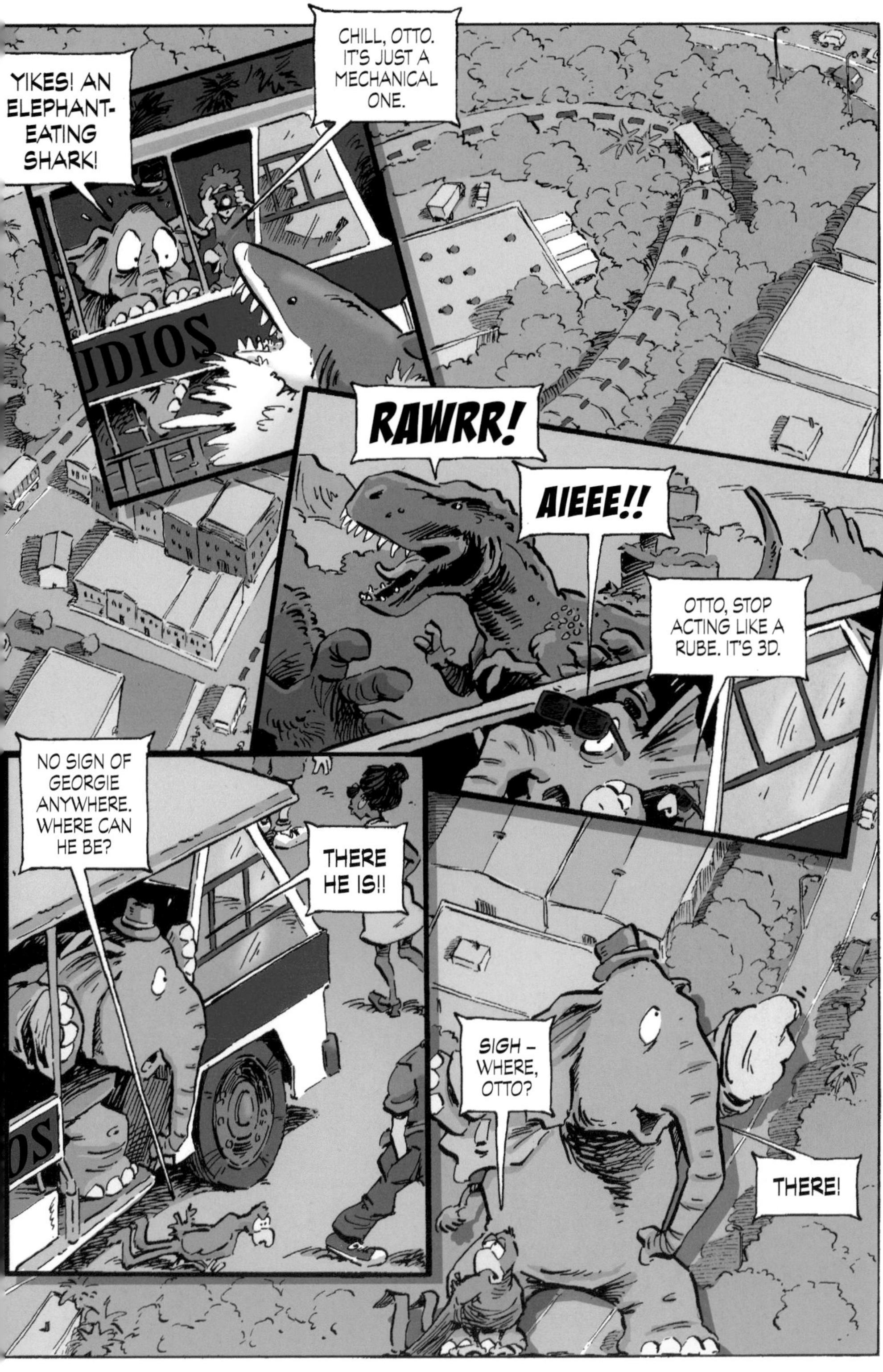
YIKES! AN ELEPHANT-EATING SHARK!
CHILL, OTTO. IT'S JUST A MECHANICAL ONE.
UDIOS
RAWRR!
AIEEE!!
OTTO, STOP ACTING LIKE A RUBE. IT'S 3D.
NO SIGN OF GEORGIE ANYWHERE. WHERE CAN HE BE?
THERE HE IS!!
OS
SIGH – WHERE, OTTO?
THERE!

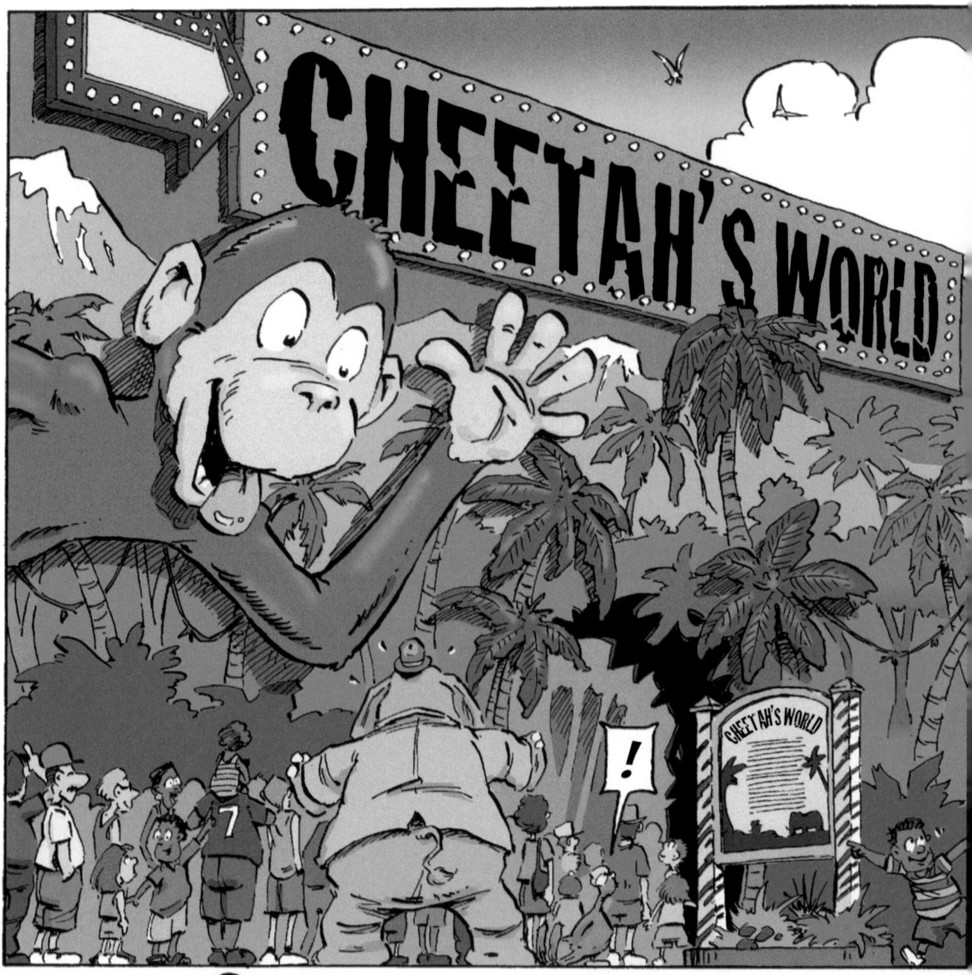
CHEETAH'S WORLD
CHEETAH'S WORLD
!

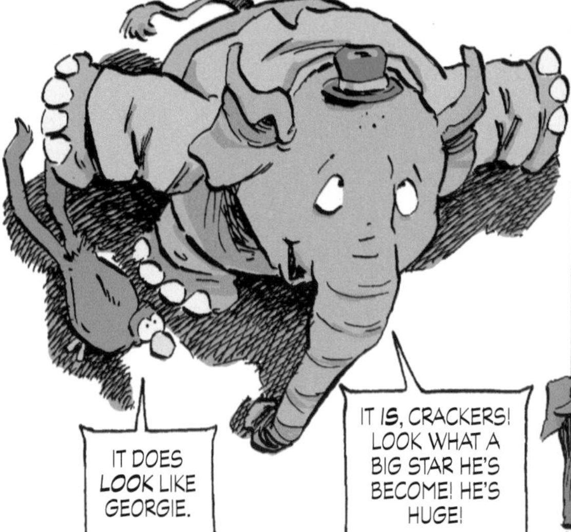
IT DOES LOOK LIKE GEORGIE.
IT IS, CRACKERS! LOOK WHAT A BIG STAR HE'S BECOME! HE'S HUGE!

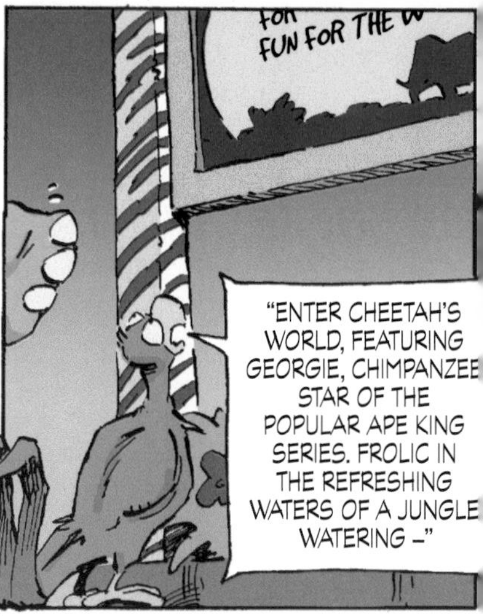
FUN FOR THE
"ENTER CHEETAH'S WORLD, FEATURING GEORGIE, CHIMPANZEE STAR OF THE POPULAR APE KING SERIES. FROLIC IN THE REFRESHING WATERS OF A JUNGLE WATERING –"

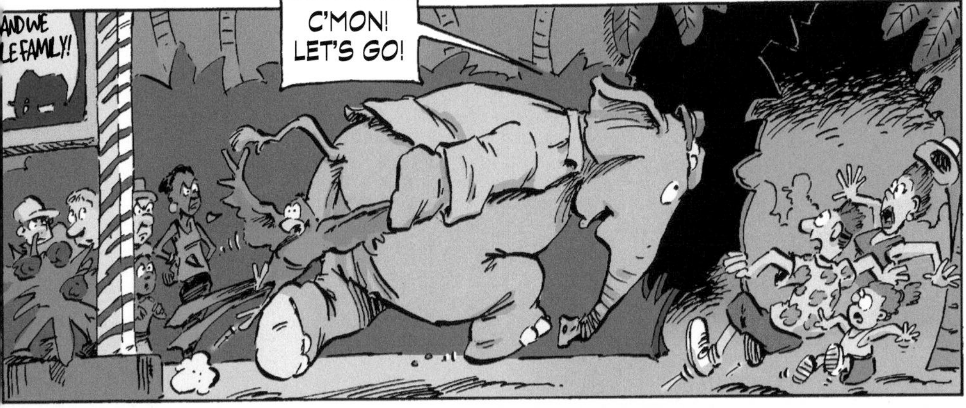
C'MON! LET'S GO!

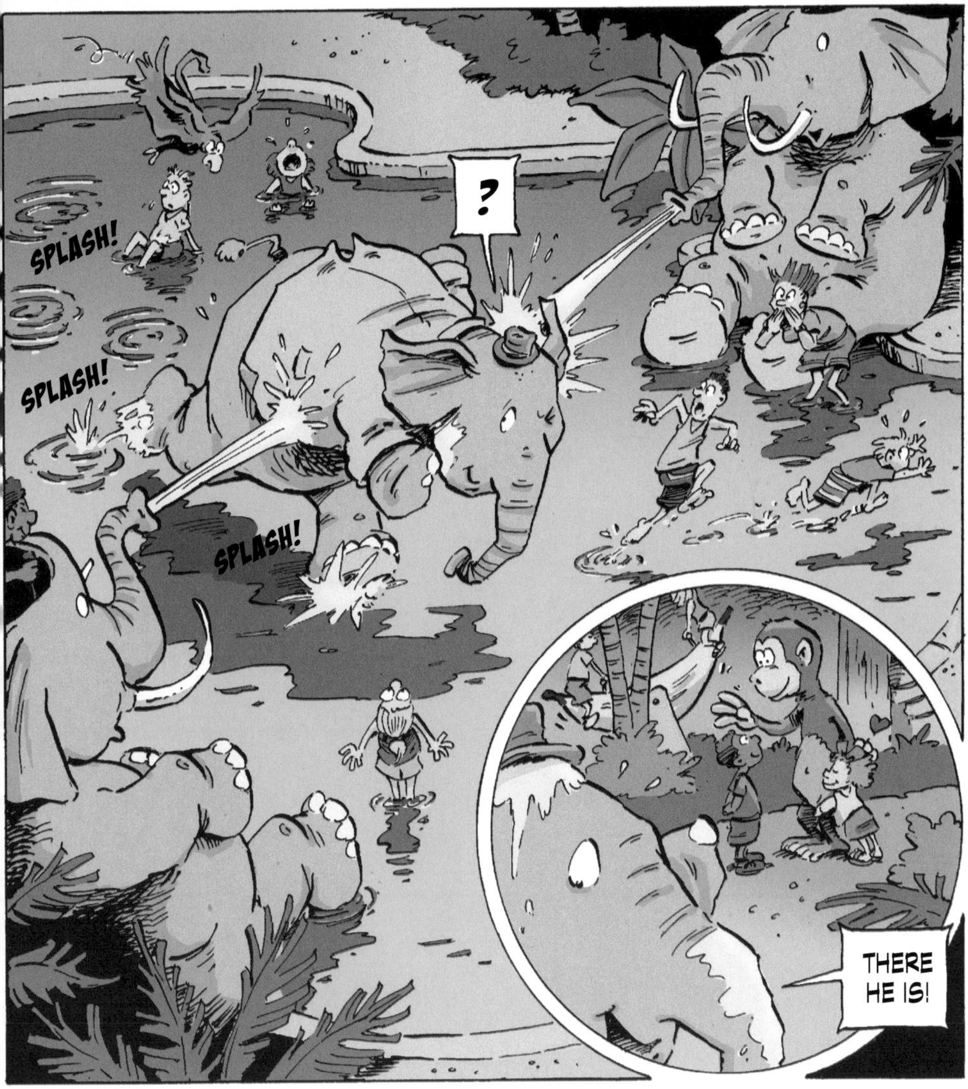
?
SPLASH!
SPLASH!
SPLASH!
THERE HE IS!

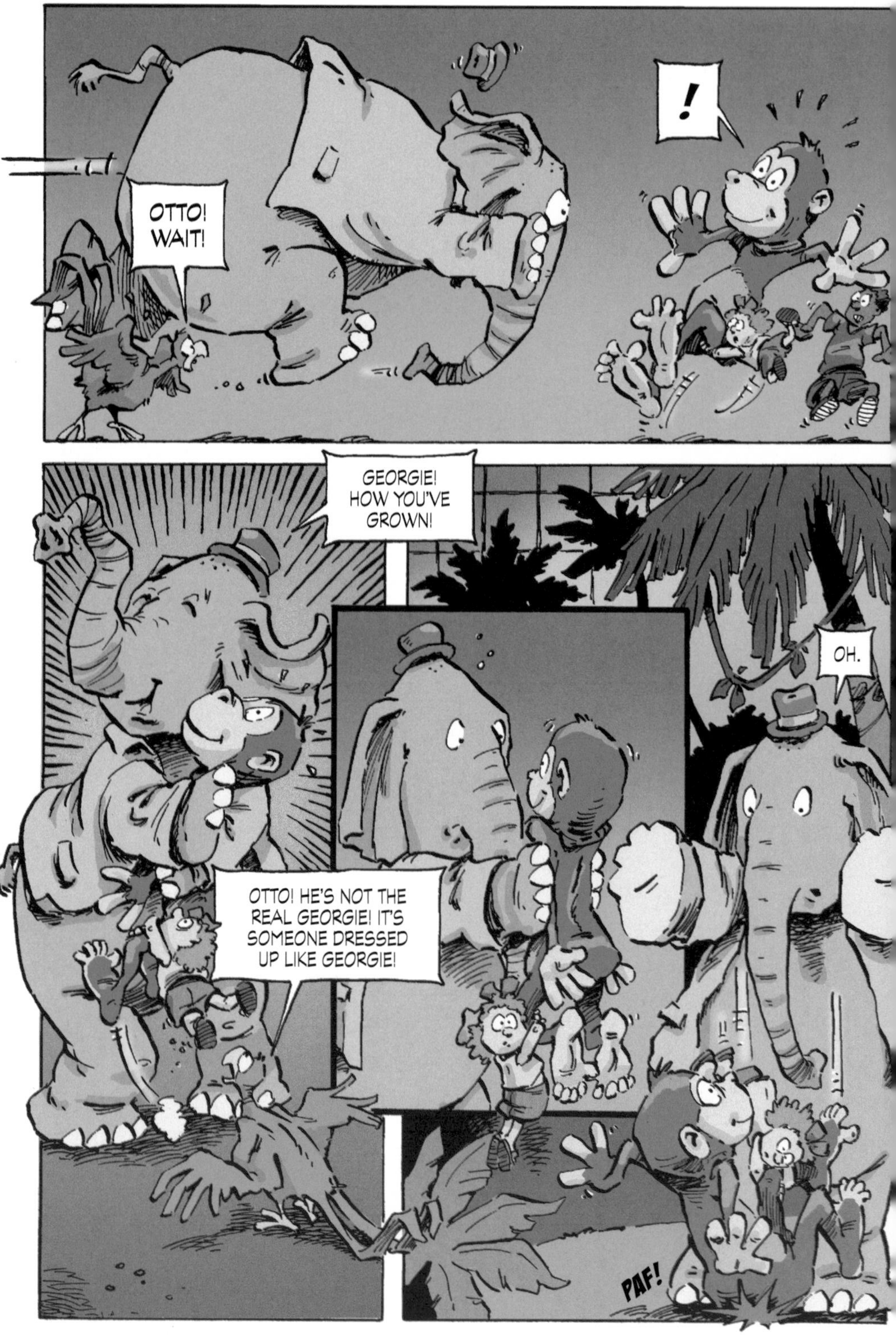
OTTO! WAIT!
!
GEORGIE! HOW YOU'VE GROWN!
OTTO! HE'S NOT THE REAL GEORGIE! IT'S SOMEONE DRESSED UP LIKE GEORGIE!
OH.
PAF!

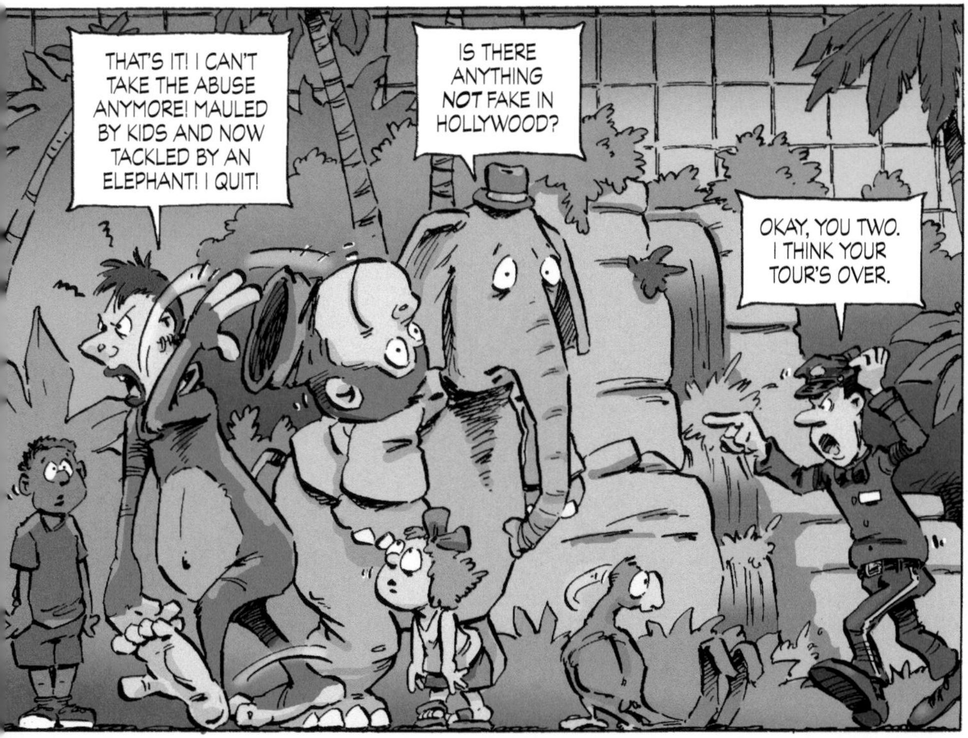
THAT'S IT! I CAN'T TAKE THE ABUSE ANYMORE! MAULED BY KIDS AND NOW TACKLED BY AN ELEPHANT! I QUIT!
IS THERE ANYTHING NOT FAKE IN HOLLYWOOD?
OKAY, YOU TWO. I THINK YOUR TOUR'S OVER.

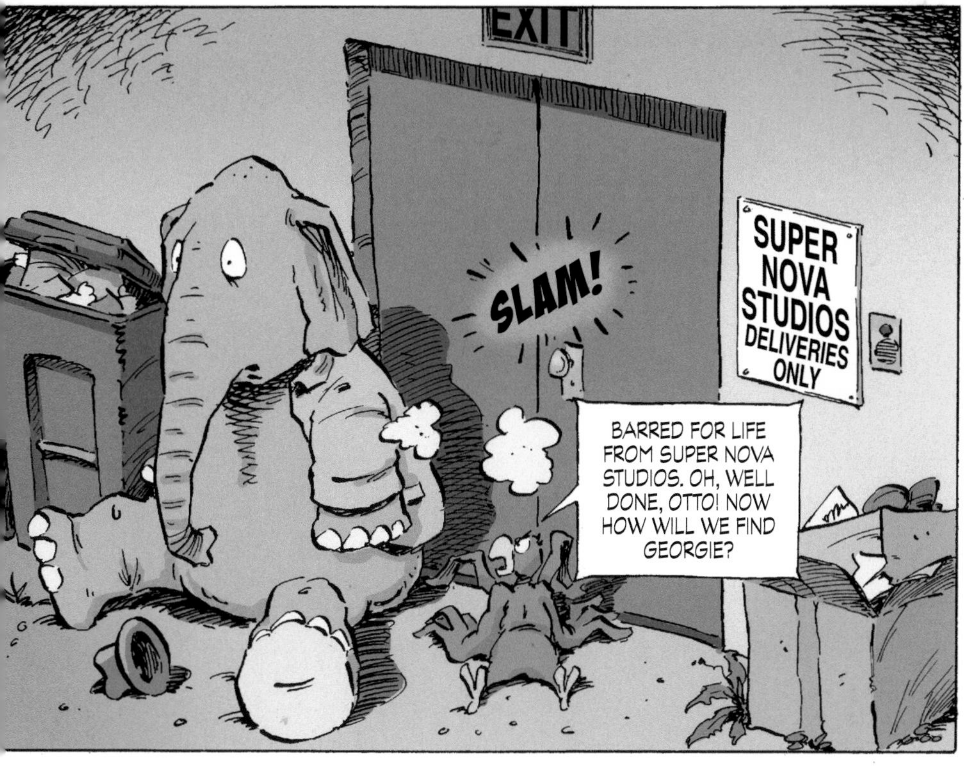
EXIT
SUPER NOVA STUDIOS DELIVERIES ONLY
SLAM!
BARRED FOR LIFE FROM SUPER NOVA STUDIOS. OH, WELL DONE, OTTO! NOW HOW WILL WE FIND GEORGIE?

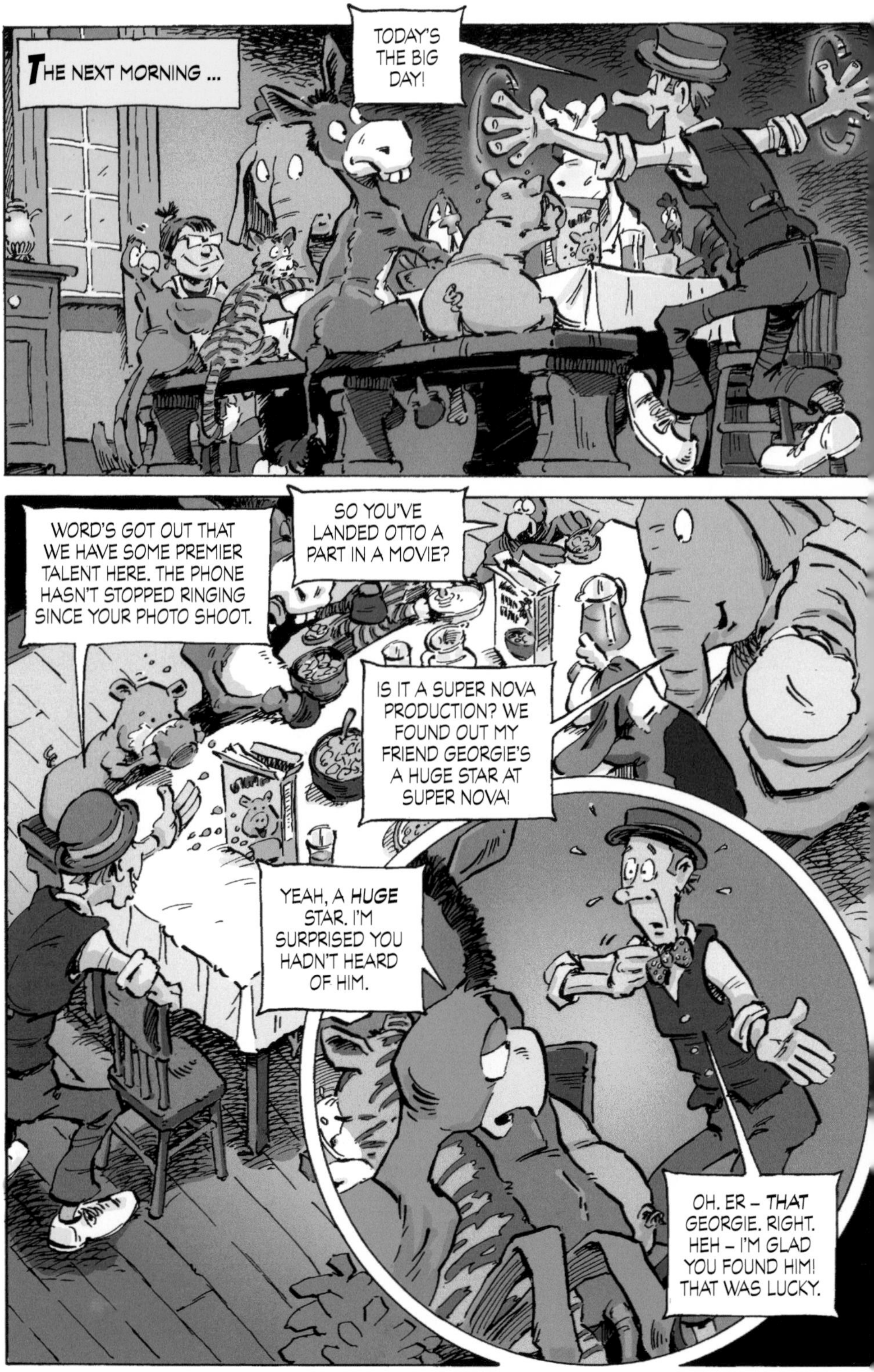
THE NEXT MORNING ...
TODAY'S THE BIG DAY!
WORD'S GOT OUT THAT WE HAVE SOME PREMIER TALENT HERE. THE PHONE HASN'T STOPPED RINGING SINCE YOUR PHOTO SHOOT.
SO YOU'VE LANDED OTTO A PART IN A MOVIE?
IS IT A SUPER NOVA PRODUCTION? WE FOUND OUT MY FRIEND GEORGIE'S A HUGE STAR AT SUPER NOVA!
YEAH, A **HUGE** STAR. I'M SURPRISED YOU HADN'T HEARD OF HIM.
OH. ER – **THAT** GEORGIE. RIGHT. HEH – I'M GLAD YOU FOUND HIM! THAT WAS LUCKY.

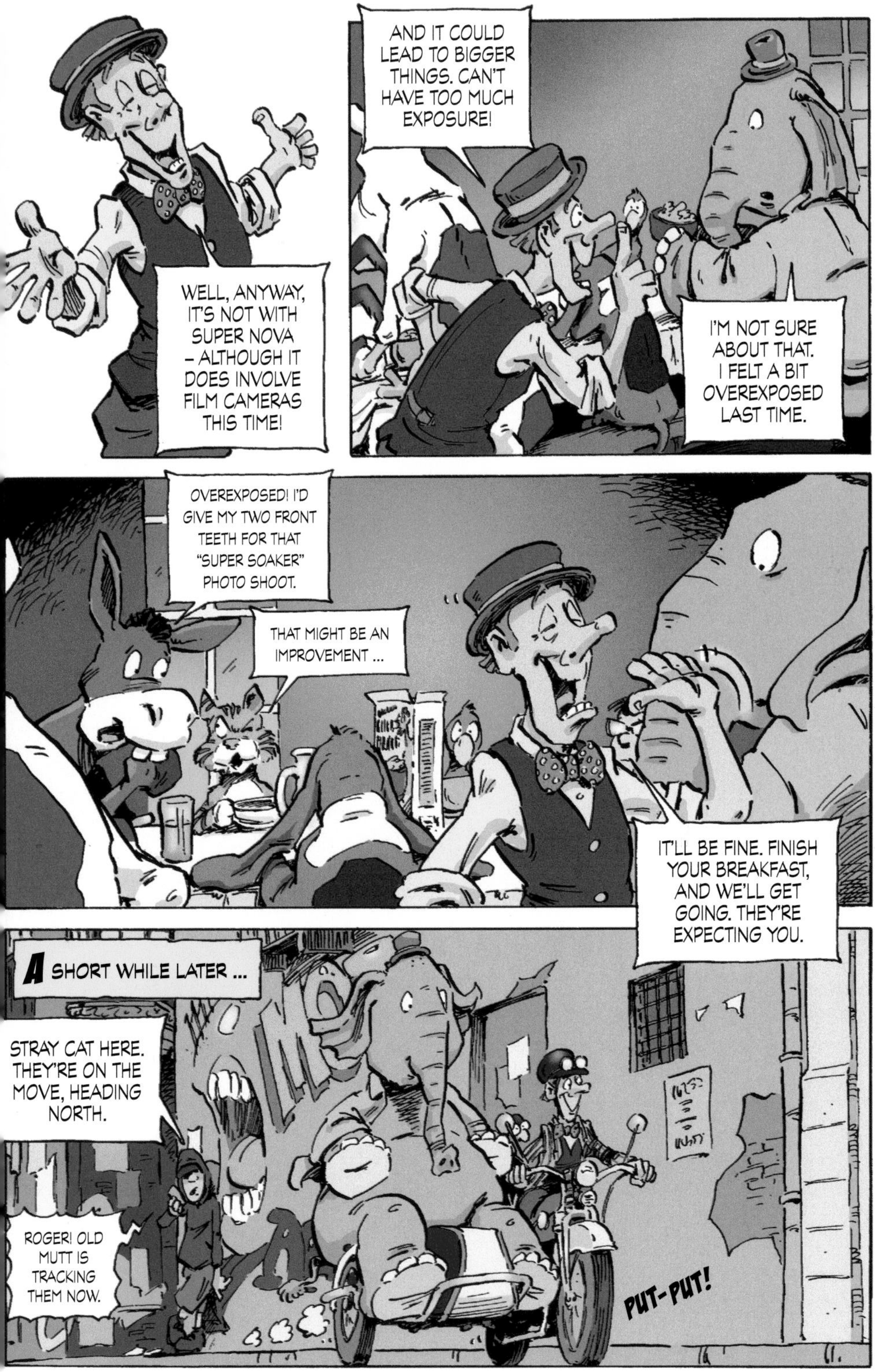
WELL, ANYWAY, IT'S NOT WITH SUPER NOVA – ALTHOUGH IT DOES INVOLVE FILM CAMERAS THIS TIME!
AND IT COULD LEAD TO BIGGER THINGS. CAN'T HAVE TOO MUCH EXPOSURE!
I'M NOT SURE ABOUT THAT. I FELT A BIT OVEREXPOSED LAST TIME.
OVEREXPOSED! I'D GIVE MY TWO FRONT TEETH FOR THAT "SUPER SOAKER" PHOTO SHOOT.
THAT MIGHT BE AN IMPROVEMENT ...
IT'LL BE FINE. FINISH YOUR BREAKFAST, AND WE'LL GET GOING. THEY'RE EXPECTING YOU.
A SHORT WHILE LATER ...
STRAY CAT HERE. THEY'RE ON THE MOVE, HEADING NORTH.
ROGER! OLD MUTT IS TRACKING THEM NOW.
PUT-PUT!

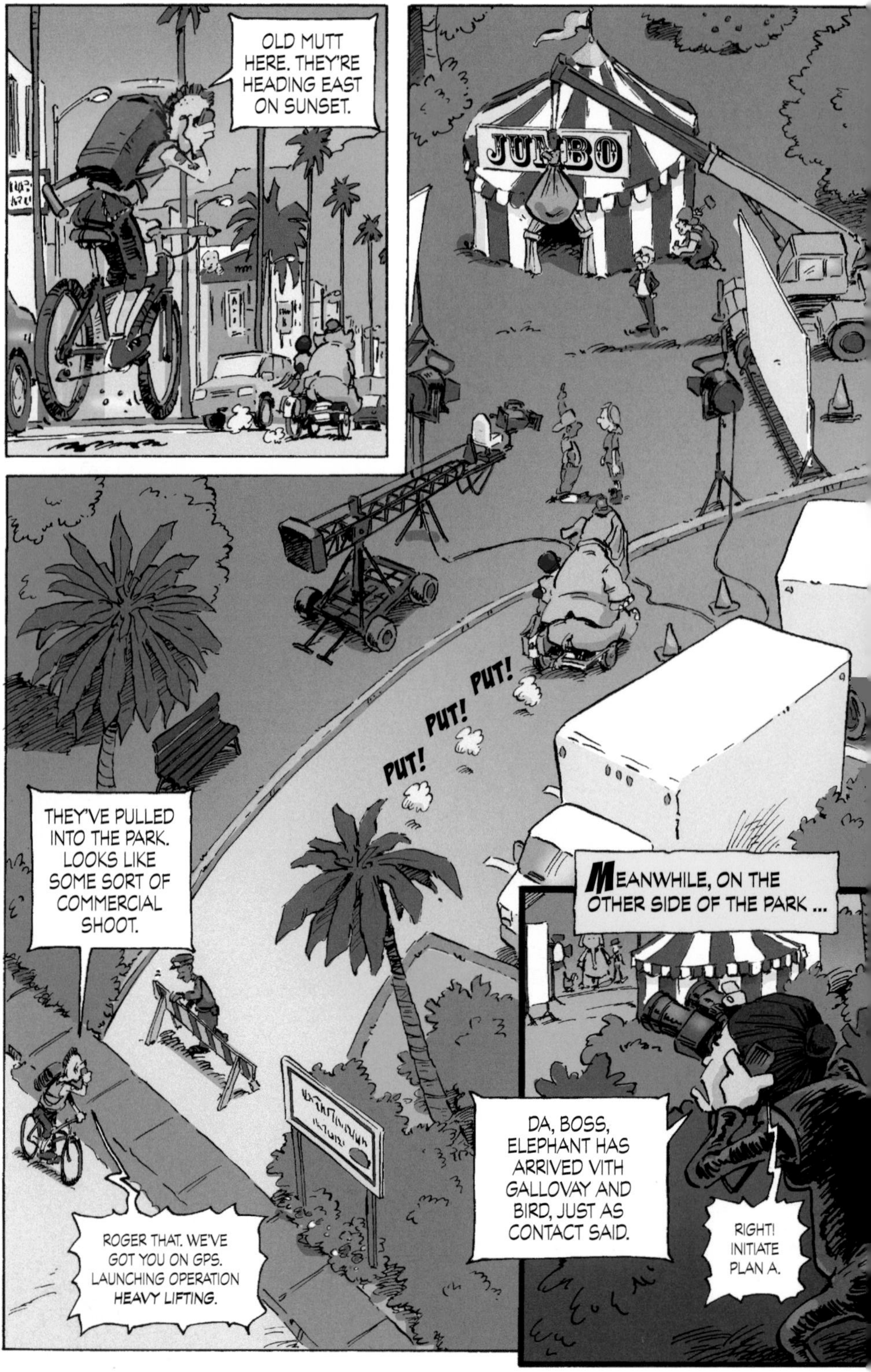
OLD MUTT HERE. THEY'RE HEADING EAST ON SUNSET.
JUMBO
PUT!
PUT!
PUT!
THEY'VE PULLED INTO THE PARK. LOOKS LIKE SOME SORT OF COMMERCIAL SHOOT.
ROGER THAT. WE'VE GOT YOU ON GPS. LAUNCHING OPERATION HEAVY LIFTING.
MEANWHILE, ON THE OTHER SIDE OF THE PARK ...
DA, BOSS, ELEPHANT HAS ARRIVED VITH GALLOVAY AND BIRD, JUST AS CONTACT SAID.
RIGHT! INITIATE PLAN A.

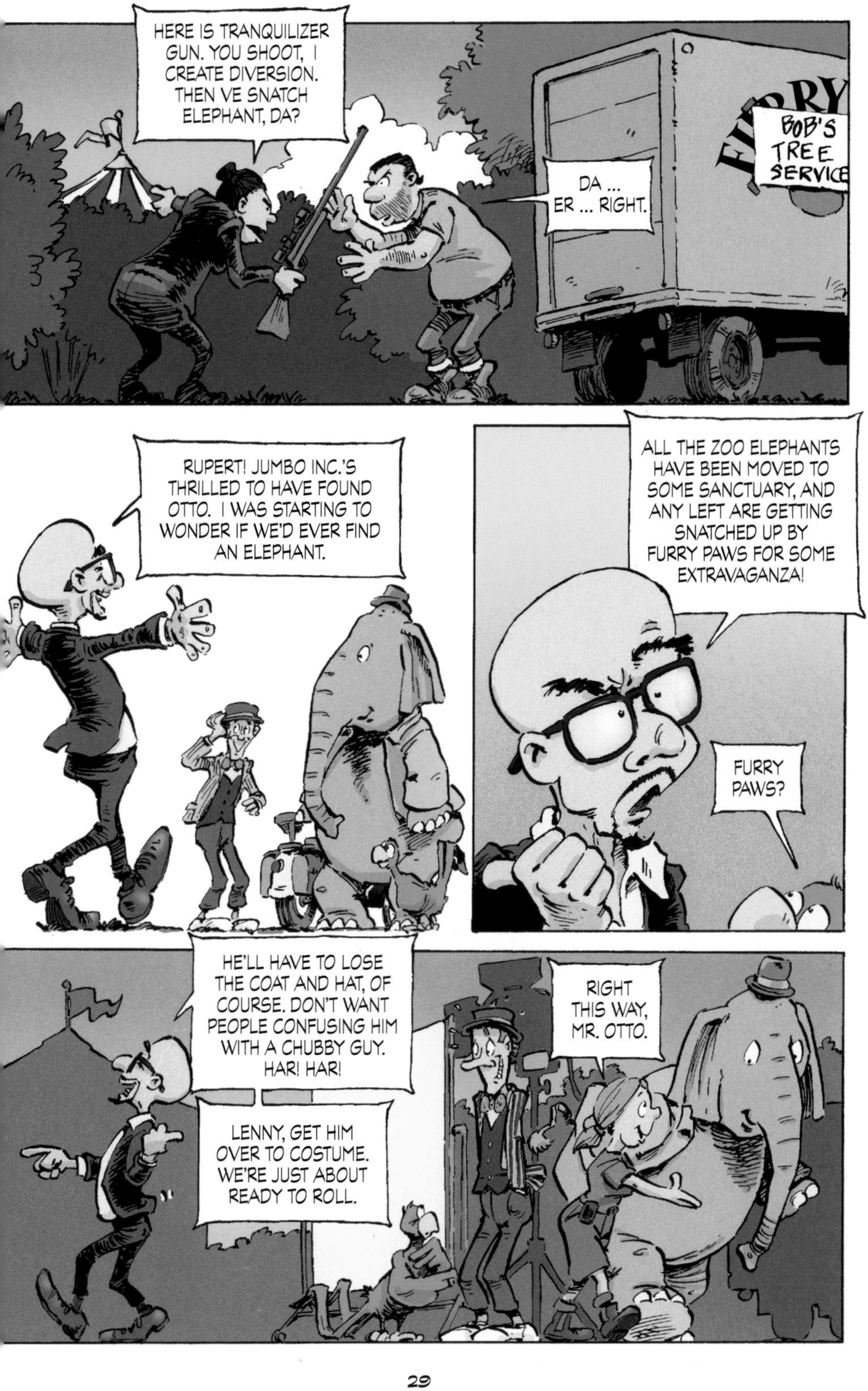
HERE IS TRANQUILIZER GUN. YOU SHOOT, I CREATE DIVERSION. THEN VE SNATCH ELEPHANT, DA?
BOB'S TREE
DA ... ER ... RIGHT.
RUPERT! JUMBO INC.'S THRILLED TO HAVE FOUND OTTO. I WAS STARTING TO WONDER IF WE'D EVER FIND AN ELEPHANT.
ALL THE ZOO ELEPHANTS HAVE BEEN MOVED TO SOME SANCTUARY, AND ANY LEFT ARE GETTING SNATCHED UP BY FURRY PAWS FOR SOME EXTRAVAGANZA!
FURRY PAWS?
HE'LL HAVE TO LOSE THE COAT AND HAT, OF COURSE. DON'T WANT PEOPLE CONFUSING HIM WITH A CHUBBY GUY. HAR! HAR!
LENNY, GET HIM OVER TO COSTUME. WE'RE JUST ABOUT READY TO ROLL.
RIGHT THIS WAY, MR. OTTO.

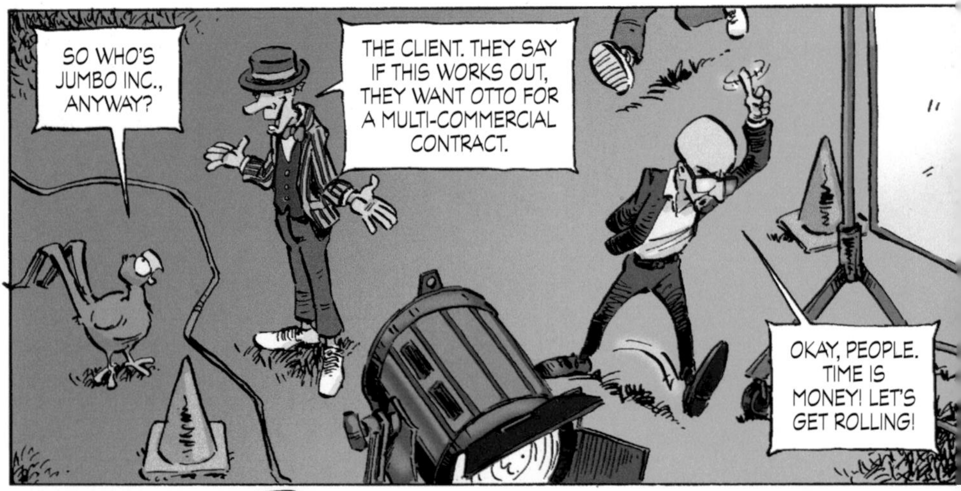
SO WHO'S JUMBO INC., ANYWAY?
THE CLIENT. THEY SAY IF THIS WORKS OUT, THEY WANT OTTO FOR A MULTI-COMMERCIAL CONTRACT.
OKAY, PEOPLE. TIME IS MONEY! LET'S GET ROLLING!

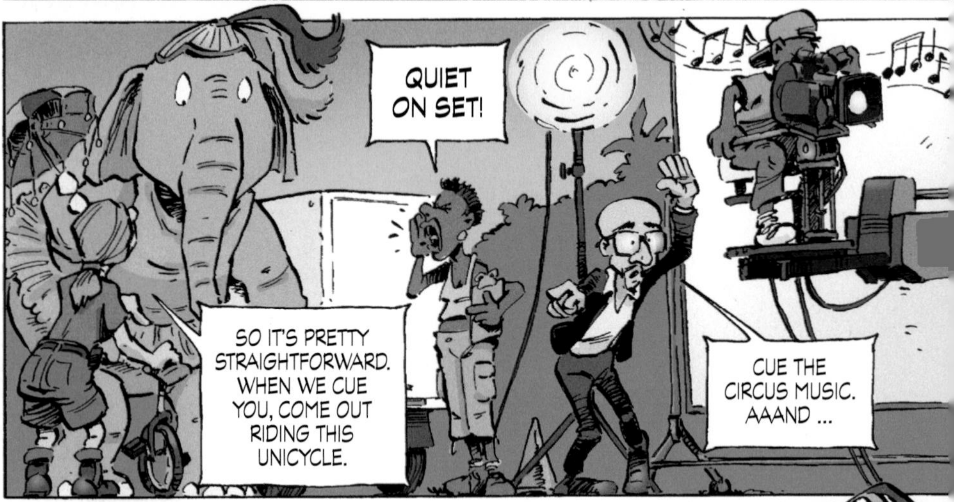
QUIET ON SET!
SO IT'S PRETTY STRAIGHTFORWARD. WHEN WE CUE YOU, COME OUT RIDING THIS UNICYCLE.
CUE THE CIRCUS MUSIC. AAAND ...

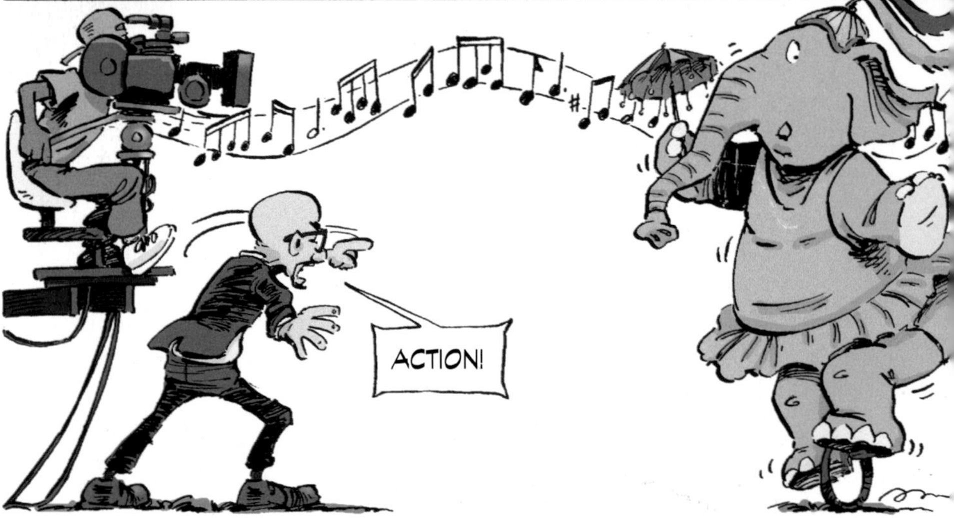
ACTION!

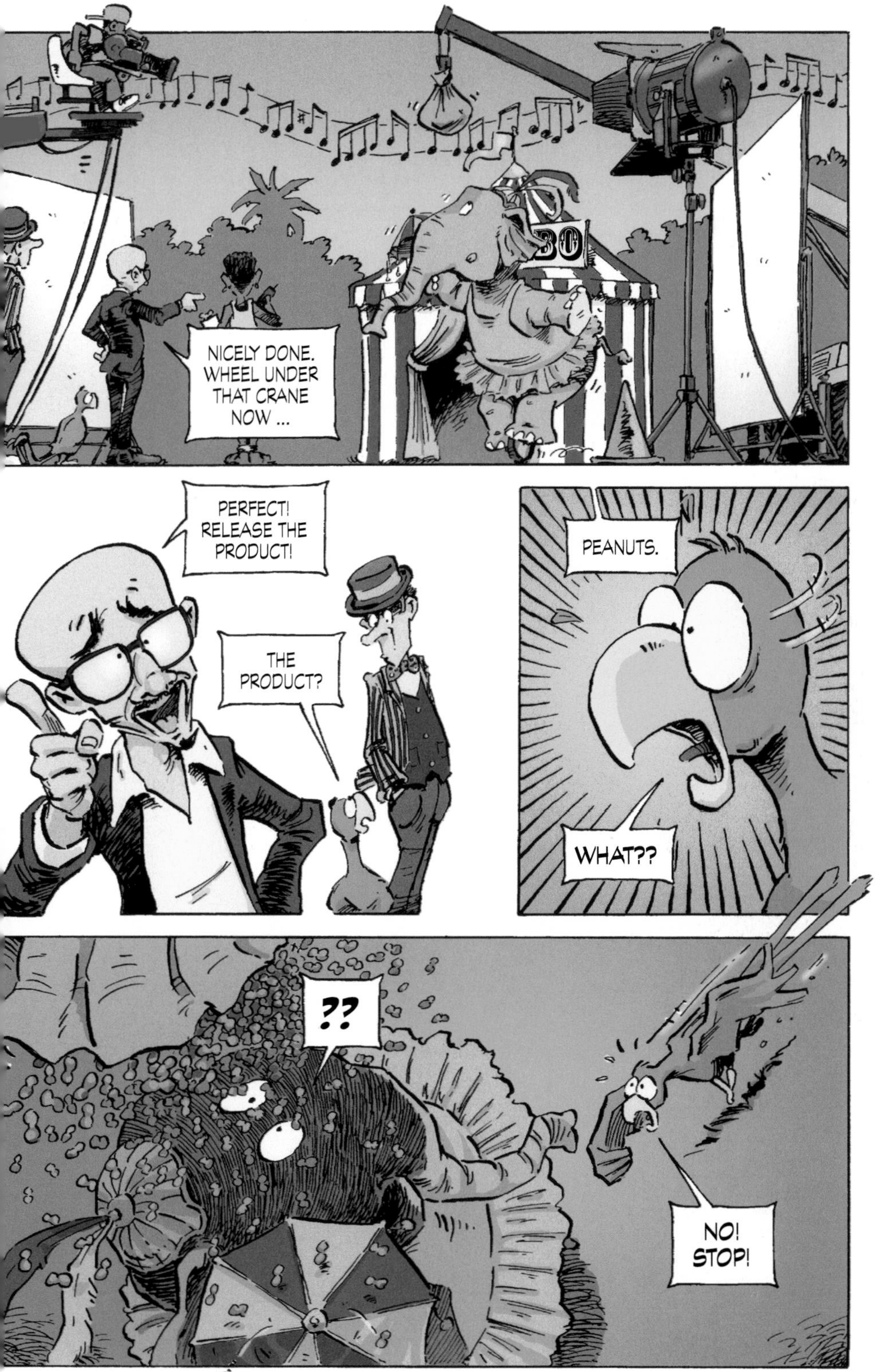
30
NICELY DONE. WHEEL UNDER THAT CRANE NOW ...
PERFECT! RELEASE THE PRODUCT!
THE PRODUCT?
PEANUTS.
WHAT??
??
NO! STOP!

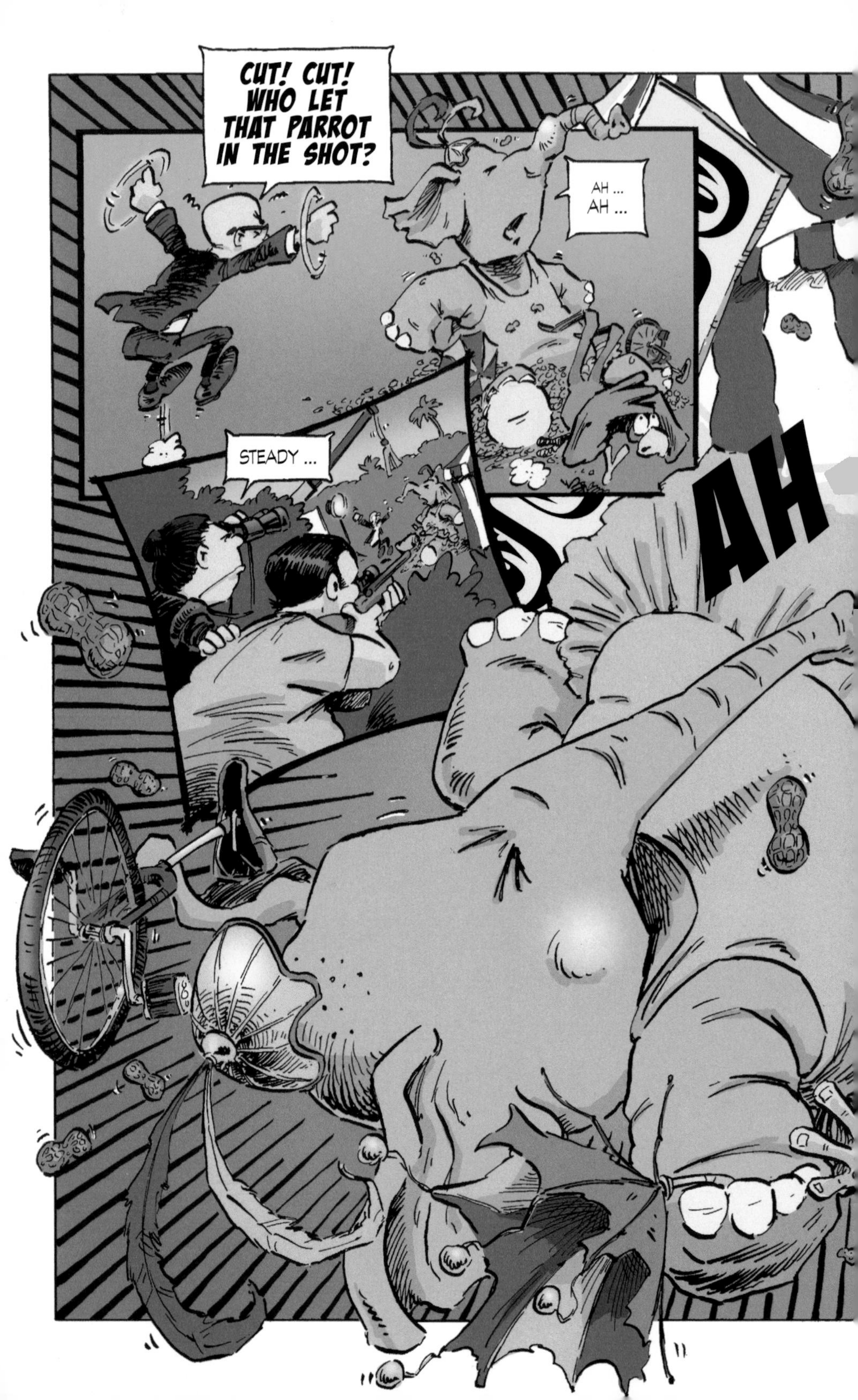
CUT! CUT! WHO LET THAT PARROT IN THE SHOT?
AH ... AH ...
STEADY ...
AH

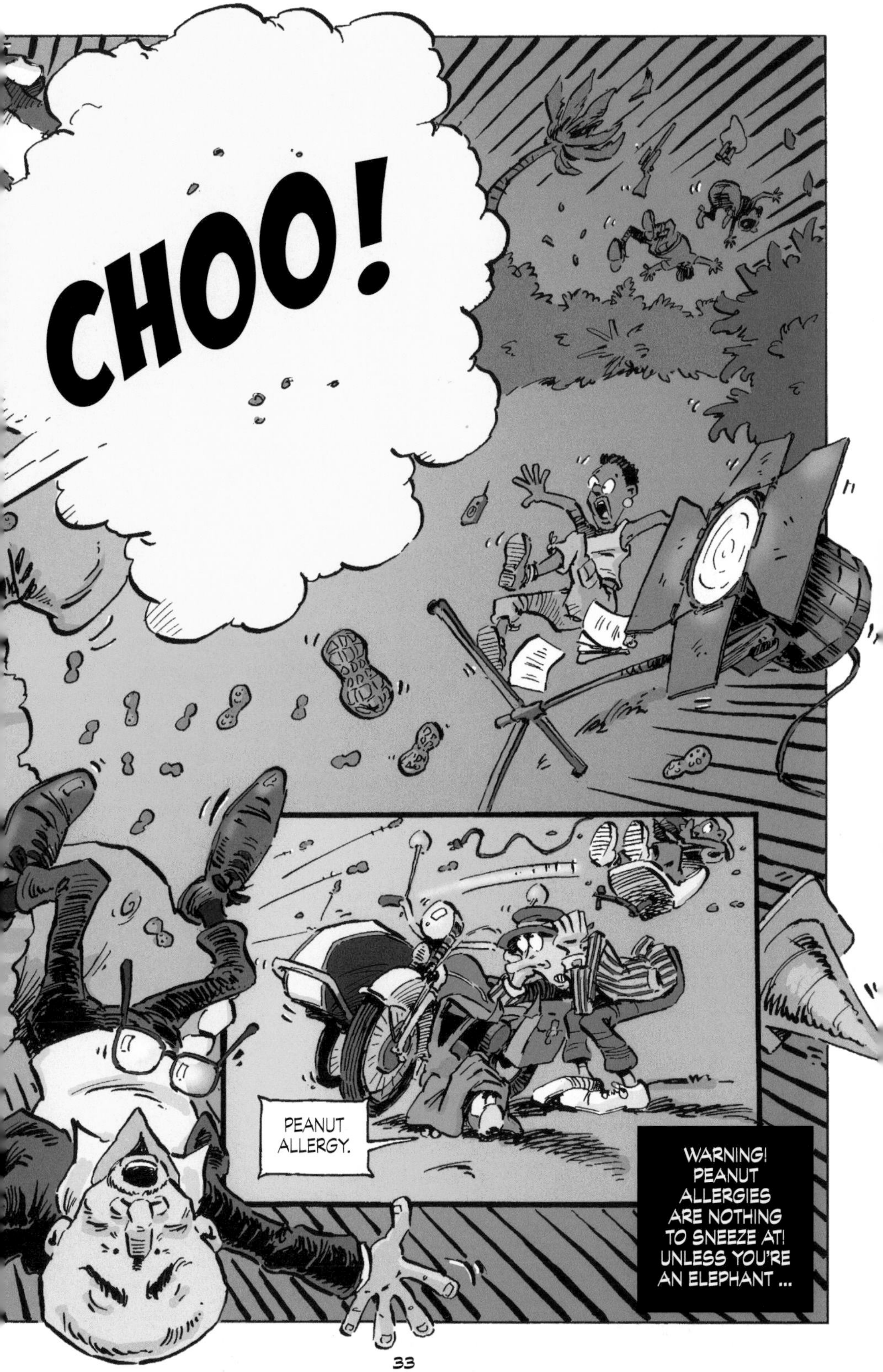
CHOO!
PEANUT ALLERGY.
WARNING! PEANUT ALLERGIES ARE NOTHING TO SNEEZE AT! UNLESS YOU'RE AN ELEPHANT ...

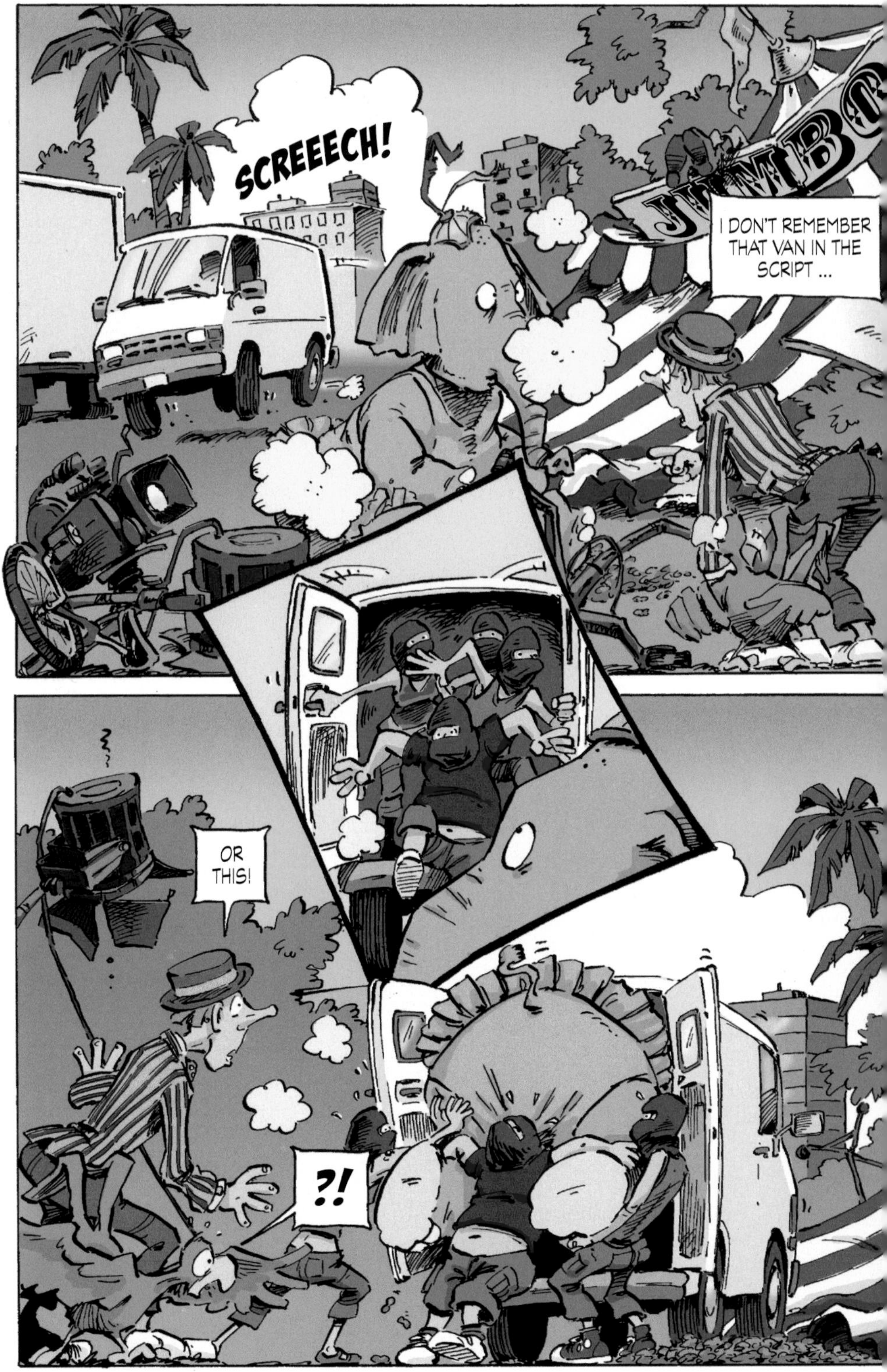
SCREEECH!
I DON'T REMEMBER THAT VAN IN THE SCRIPT ...
OR THIS!
?!

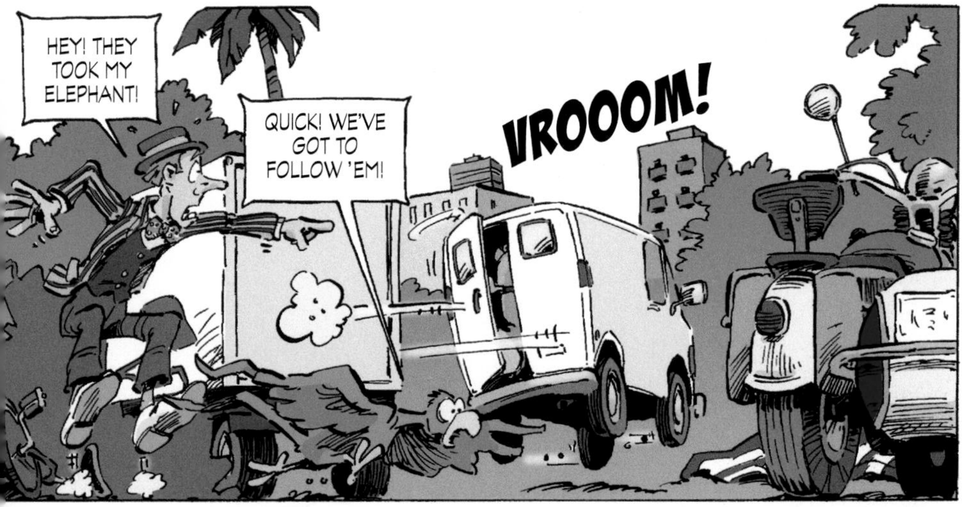
HEY! THEY TOOK MY ELEPHANT!
QUICK! WE'VE GOT TO FOLLOW 'EM!
VROOOM!

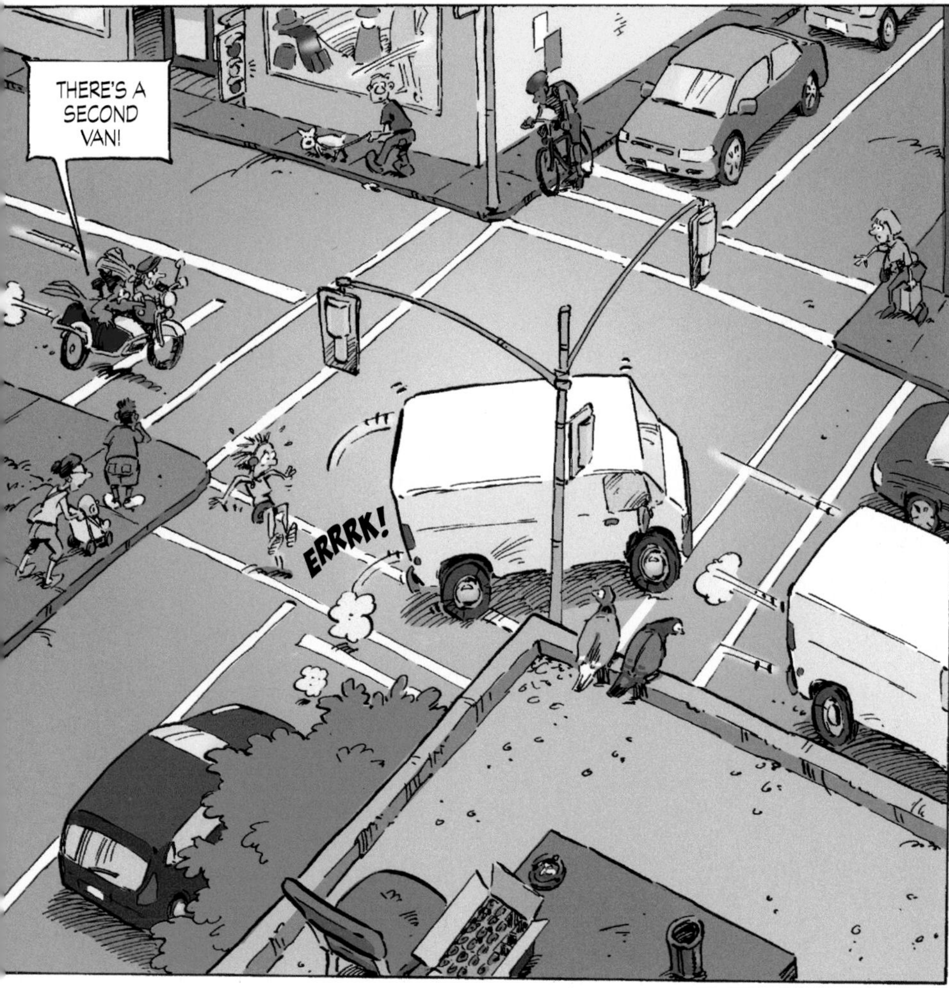
THERE'S A SECOND VAN!
ERRRK!

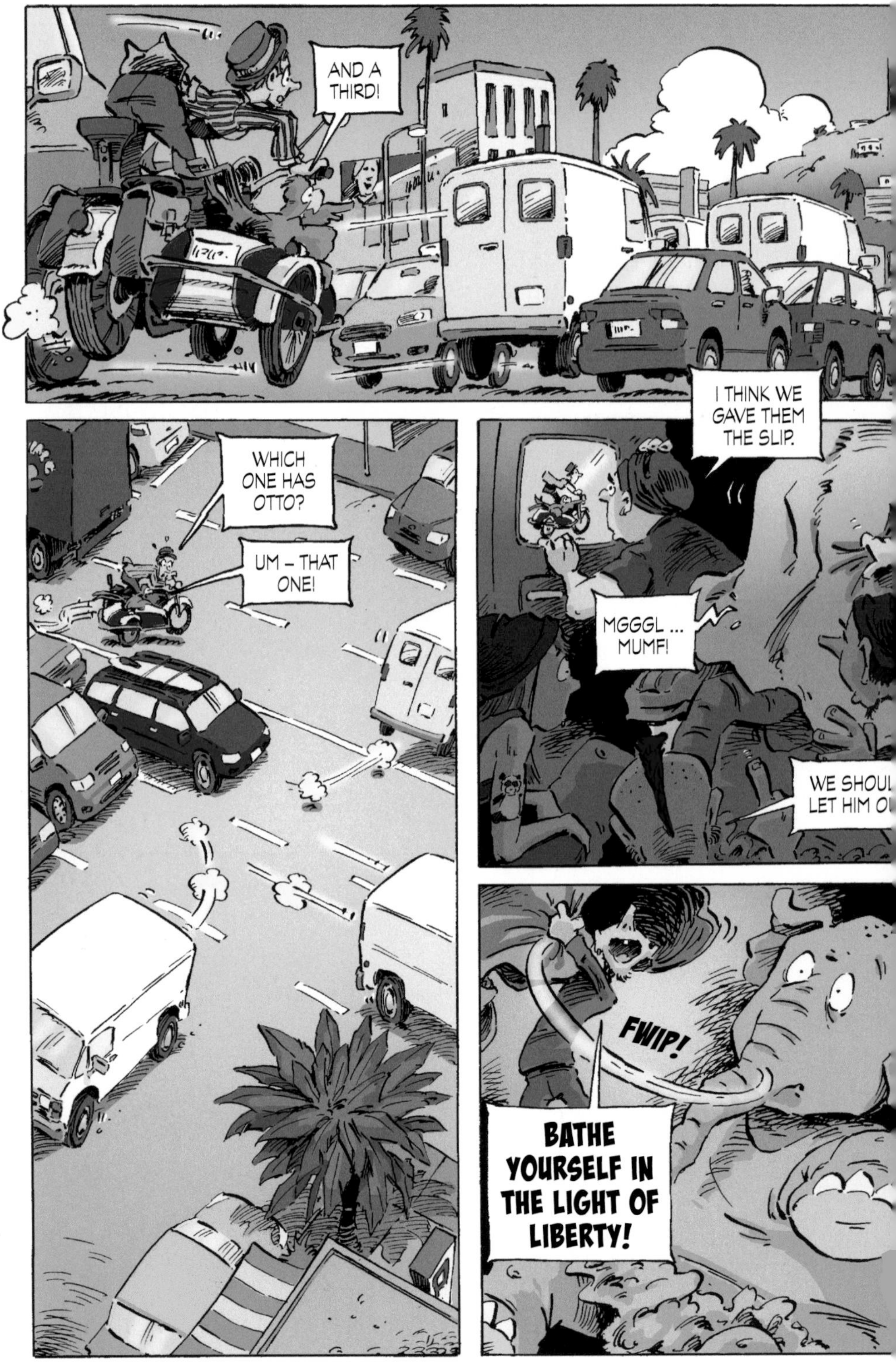
AND A THIRD!
WHICH ONE HAS OTTO?
UM – THAT ONE!
I THINK WE GAVE THEM THE SLIP.
MGGGL ... MUMF!
WE SHOUL LET HIM O
FWIP!
BATHE YOURSELF IN THE LIGHT OF LIBERTY!

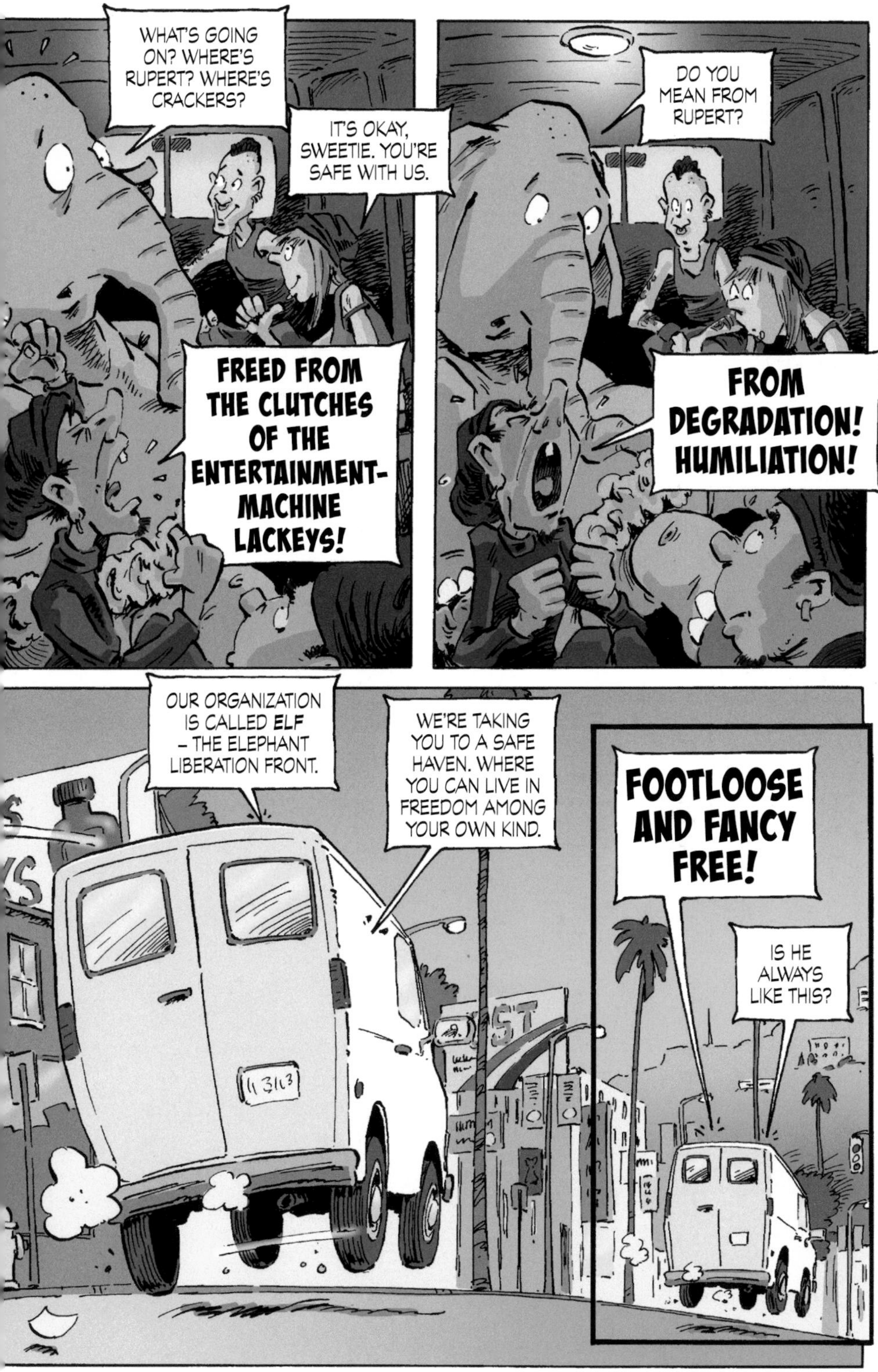
WHAT'S GOING ON? WHERE'S RUPERT? WHERE'S CRACKERS?
IT'S OKAY, SWEETIE. YOU'RE SAFE WITH US.
FREED FROM THE CLUTCHES OF THE ENTERTAINMENT-MACHINE LACKEYS!
DO YOU MEAN FROM RUPERT?
FROM DEGRADATION! HUMILIATION!
OUR ORGANIZATION IS CALLED ELF – THE ELEPHANT LIBERATION FRONT.
WE'RE TAKING YOU TO A SAFE HAVEN. WHERE YOU CAN LIVE IN FREEDOM AMONG YOUR OWN KIND.
FOOTLOOSE AND FANCY FREE!
IS HE ALWAYS LIKE THIS?

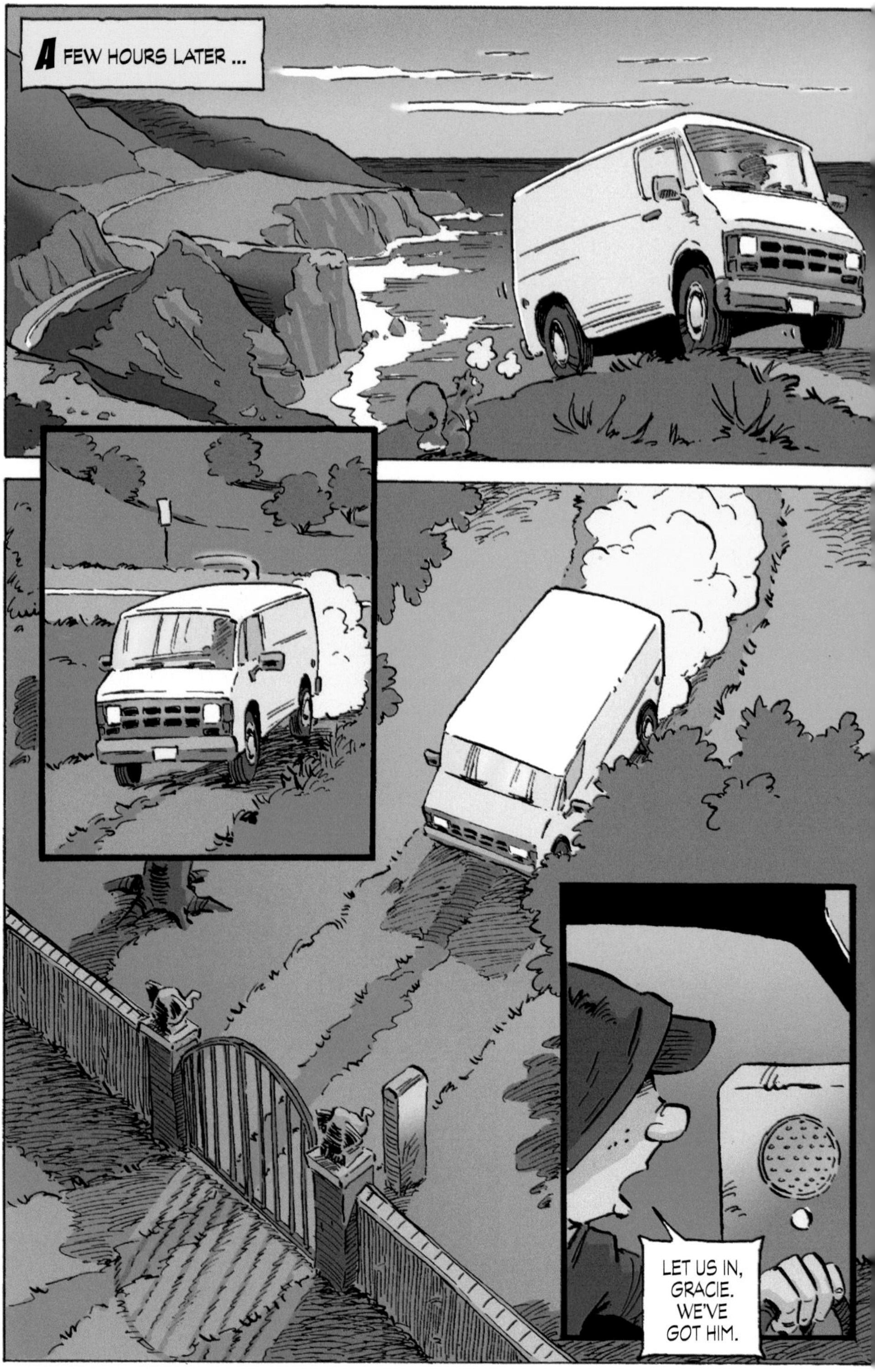
A FEW HOURS LATER ...
LET US IN, GRACIE. WE'VE GOT HIM.

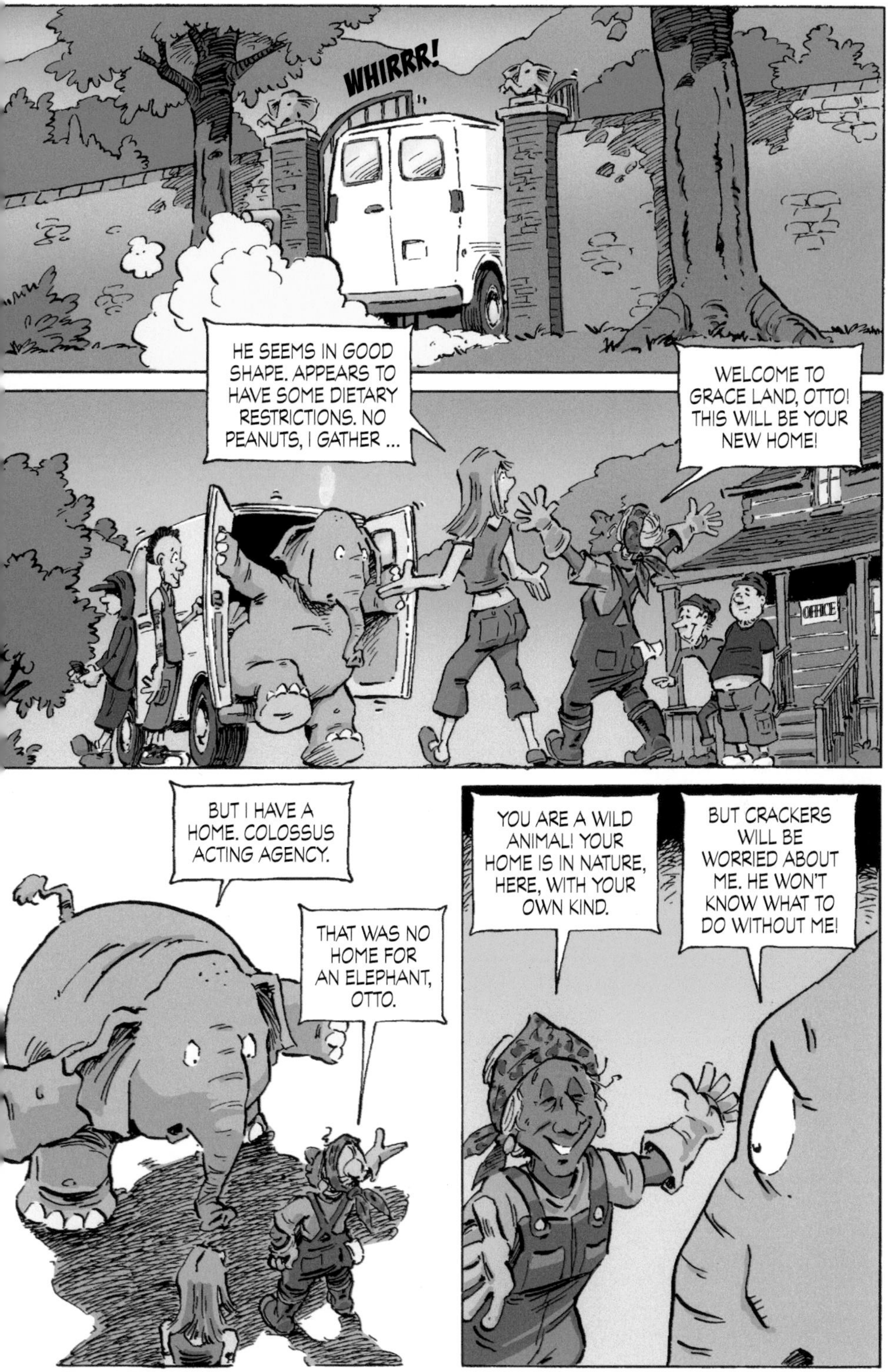

WHIRRR!
HE SEEMS IN GOOD SHAPE. APPEARS TO HAVE SOME DIETARY RESTRICTIONS. NO PEANUTS, I GATHER ...
WELCOME TO GRACE LAND, OTTO! THIS WILL BE YOUR NEW HOME!
OFFICE
BUT I HAVE A HOME. COLOSSUS ACTING AGENCY.
THAT WAS NO HOME FOR AN ELEPHANT, OTTO.
YOU ARE A WILD ANIMAL! YOUR HOME IS IN NATURE, HERE, WITH YOUR OWN KIND.
BUT CRACKERS WILL BE WORRIED ABOUT ME. HE WON'T KNOW WHAT TO DO WITHOUT ME!

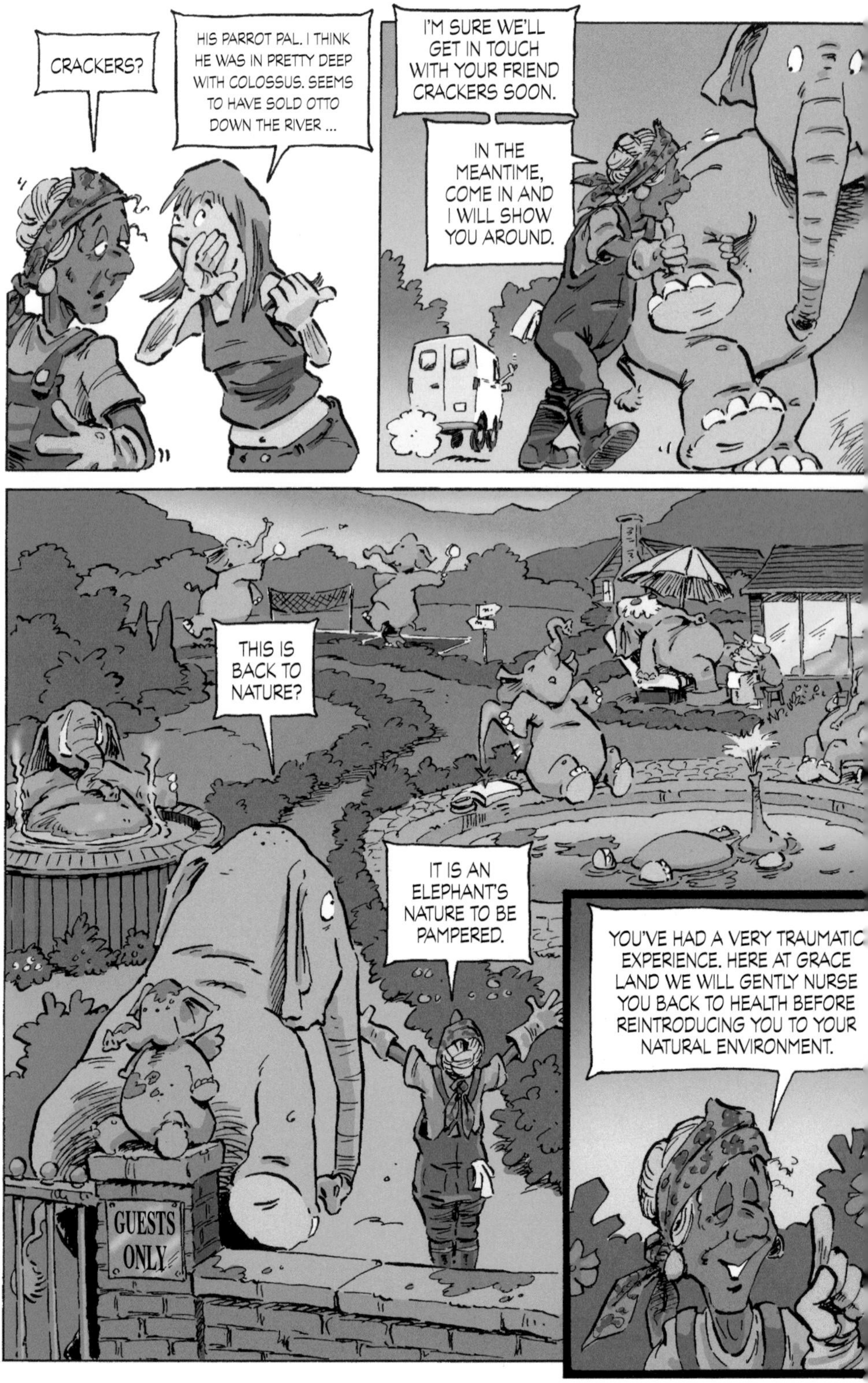
CRACKERS?
HIS PARROT PAL. I THINK HE WAS IN PRETTY DEEP WITH COLOSSUS. SEEMS TO HAVE SOLD OTTO DOWN THE RIVER ...
I'M SURE WE'LL GET IN TOUCH WITH YOUR FRIEND CRACKERS SOON.
IN THE MEANTIME, COME IN AND I WILL SHOW YOU AROUND.
THIS IS BACK TO NATURE?
IT IS AN ELEPHANT'S NATURE TO BE PAMPERED.
GUESTS ONLY
YOU'VE HAD A VERY TRAUMATIC EXPERIENCE. HERE AT GRACE LAND WE WILL GENTLY NURSE YOU BACK TO HEALTH BEFORE REINTRODUCING YOU TO YOUR NATURAL ENVIRONMENT.

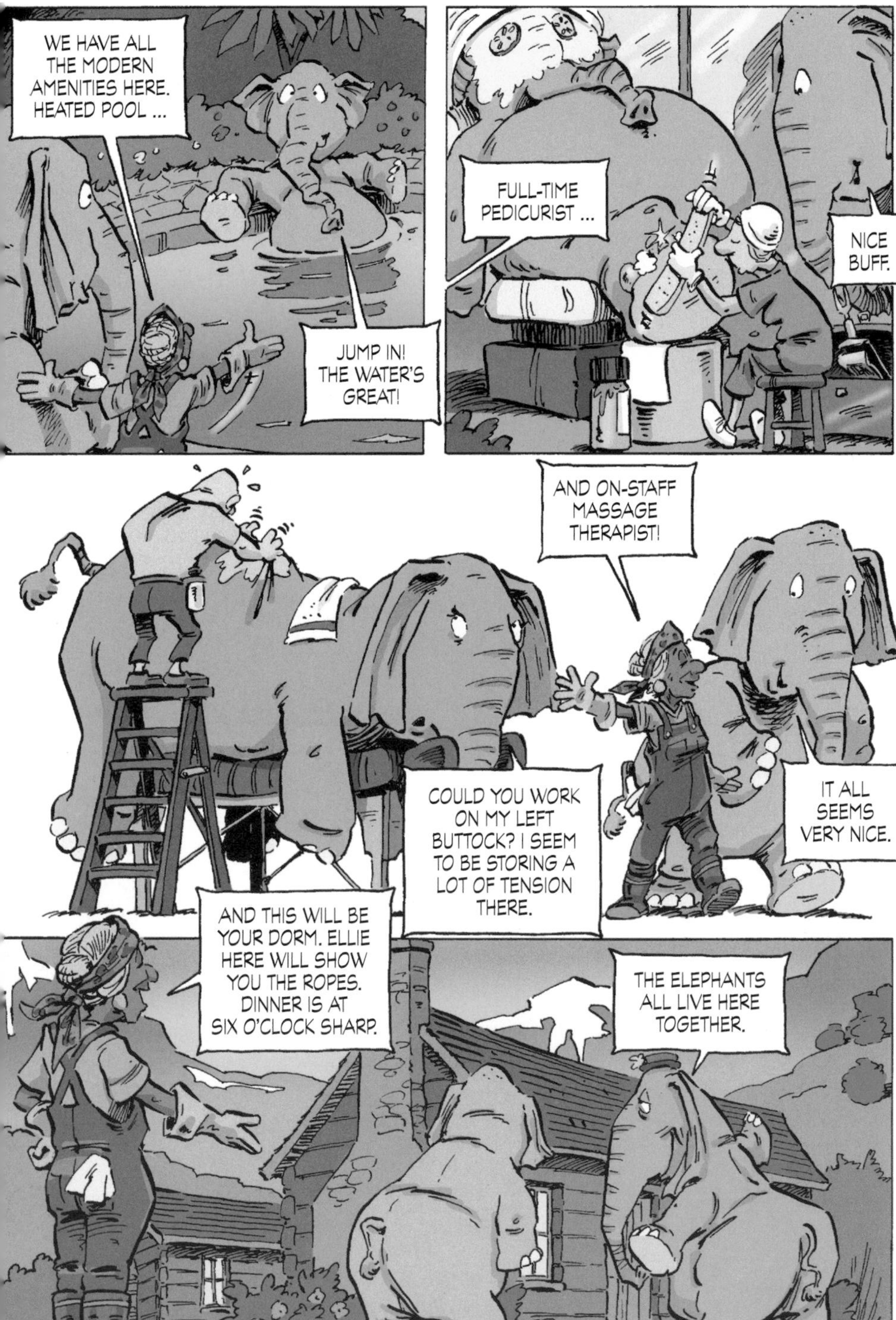
WE HAVE ALL THE MODERN AMENITIES HERE. HEATED POOL ...
JUMP IN! THE WATER'S GREAT!
FULL-TIME PEDICURIST ...
NICE BUFF.
AND ON-STAFF MASSAGE THERAPIST!
COULD YOU WORK ON MY LEFT BUTTOCK? I SEEM TO BE STORING A LOT OF TENSION THERE.
IT ALL SEEMS VERY NICE.
AND THIS WILL BE YOUR DORM. ELLIE HERE WILL SHOW YOU THE ROPES. DINNER IS AT SIX O'CLOCK SHARP.
THE ELEPHANTS ALL LIVE HERE TOGETHER.

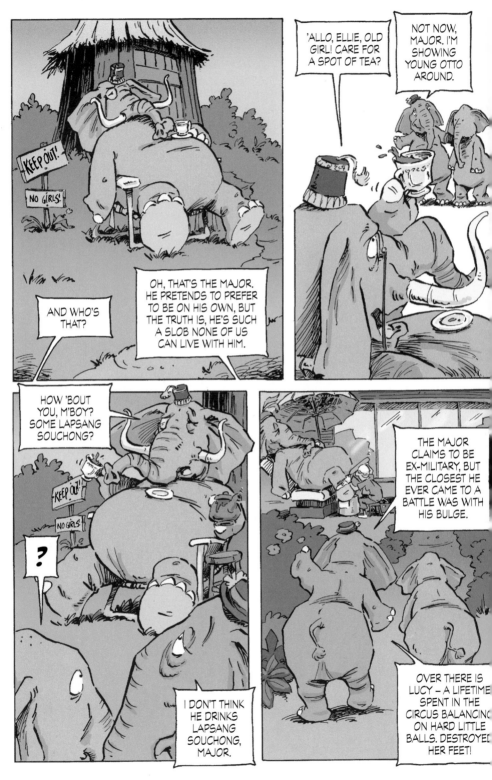

42

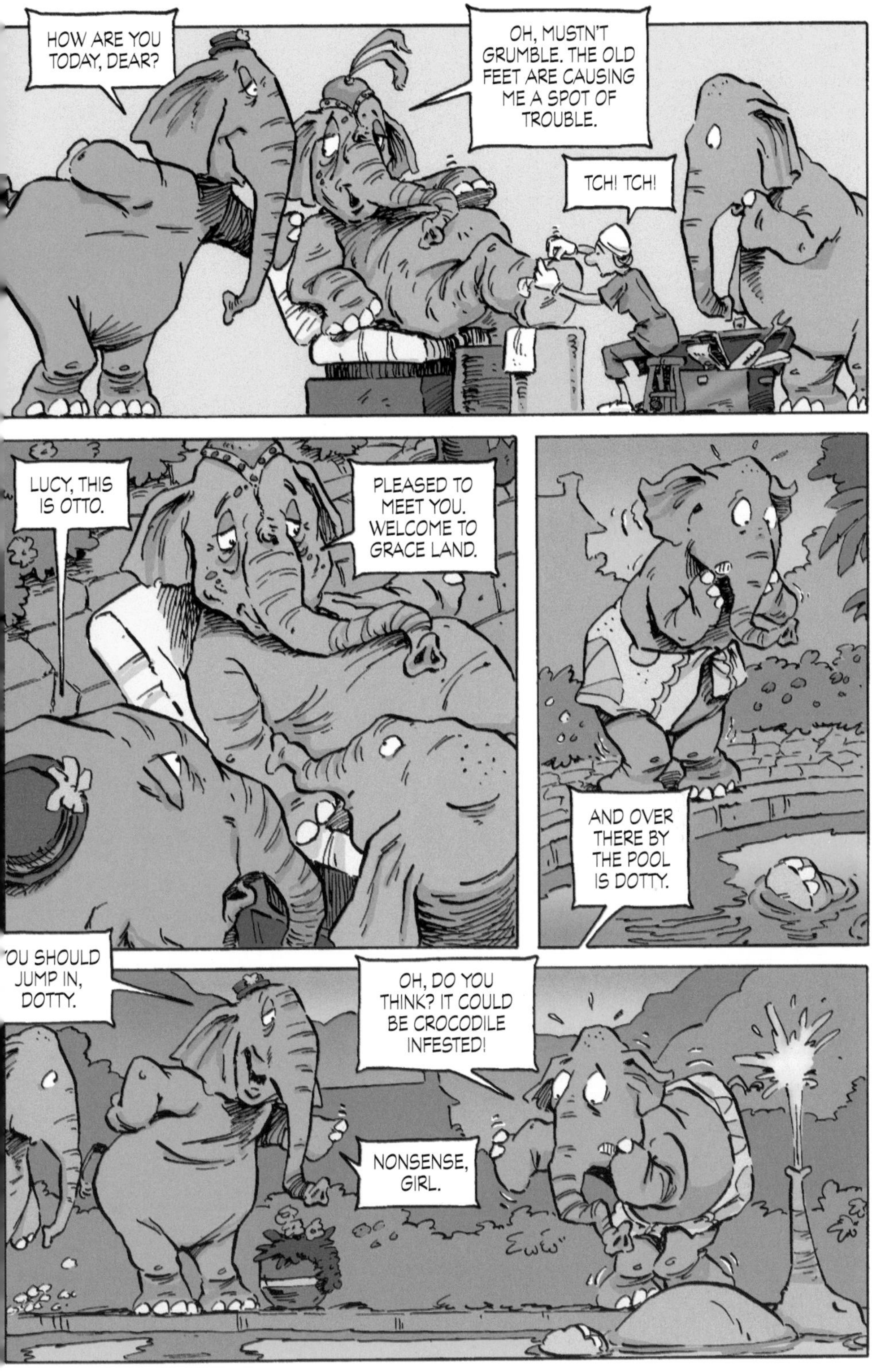
HOW ARE YOU TODAY, DEAR?
OH, MUSTN'T GRUMBLE. THE OLD FEET ARE CAUSING ME A SPOT OF TROUBLE.
TCH! TCH!
LUCY, THIS IS OTTO.
PLEASED TO MEET YOU. WELCOME TO GRACE LAND.
AND OVER THERE BY THE POOL IS DOTTY.
OU SHOULD JUMP IN, DOTTY.
OH, DO YOU THINK? IT COULD BE CROCODILE INFESTED!
NONSENSE, GIRL.

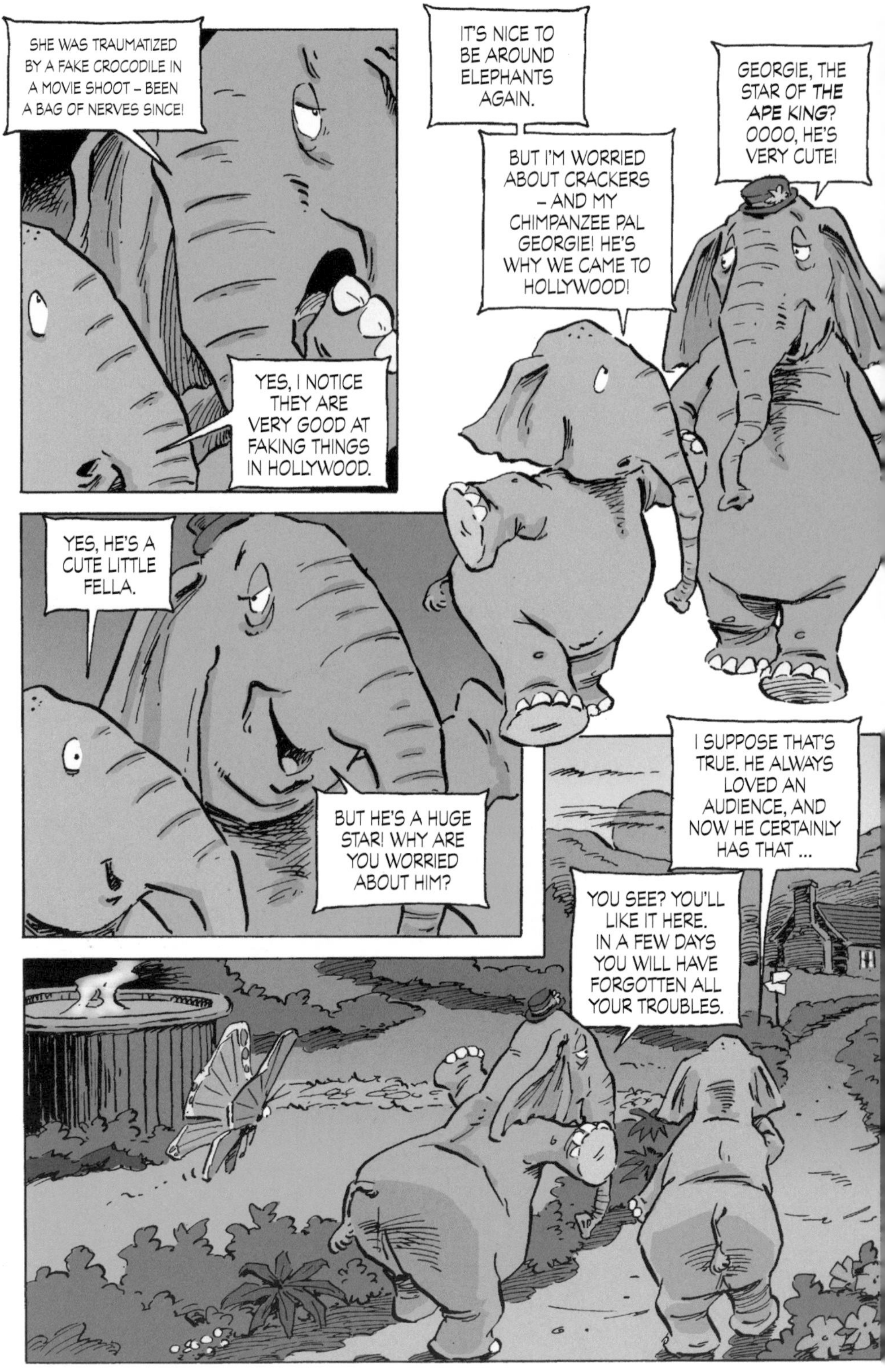
SHE WAS TRAUMATIZED BY A FAKE CROCODILE IN A MOVIE SHOOT – BEEN A BAG OF NERVES SINCE!
YES, I NOTICE THEY ARE VERY GOOD AT FAKING THINGS IN HOLLYWOOD.
IT'S NICE TO BE AROUND ELEPHANTS AGAIN.
BUT I'M WORRIED ABOUT CRACKERS – AND MY CHIMPANZEE PAL GEORGIE! HE'S WHY WE CAME TO HOLLYWOOD!
GEORGIE, THE STAR OF THE APE KING? OOOO, HE'S VERY CUTE!
YES, HE'S A CUTE LITTLE FELLA.
BUT HE'S A HUGE STAR! WHY ARE YOU WORRIED ABOUT HIM?
I SUPPOSE THAT'S TRUE. HE ALWAYS LOVED AN AUDIENCE, AND NOW HE CERTAINLY HAS THAT ...
YOU SEE? YOU'LL LIKE IT HERE. IN A FEW DAYS YOU WILL HAVE FORGOTTEN ALL YOUR TROUBLES.

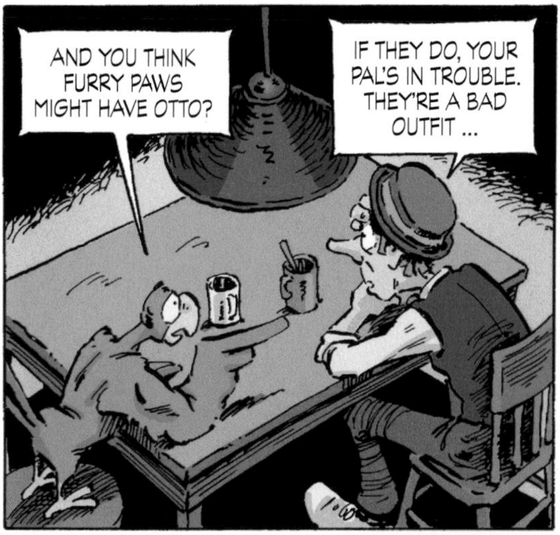
AND YOU THINK FURRY PAWS MIGHT HAVE OTTO?
IF THEY DO, YOUR PAL'S IN TROUBLE. THEY'RE A BAD OUTFIT ...

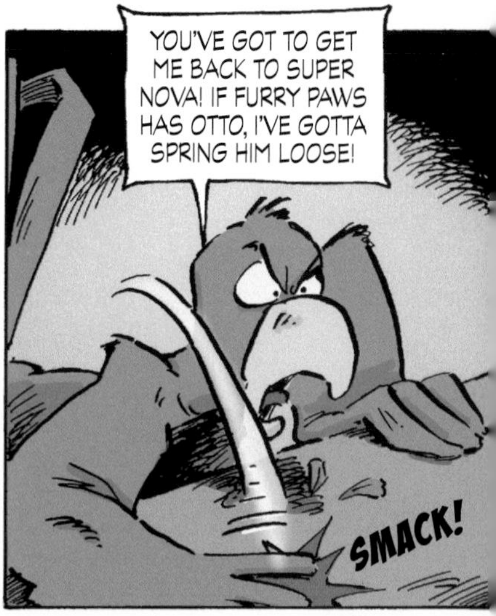
YOU'VE GOT TO GET ME BACK TO SUPER NOVA! IF FURRY PAWS HAS OTTO, I'VE GOTTA SPRING HIM LOOSE!
SMACK!

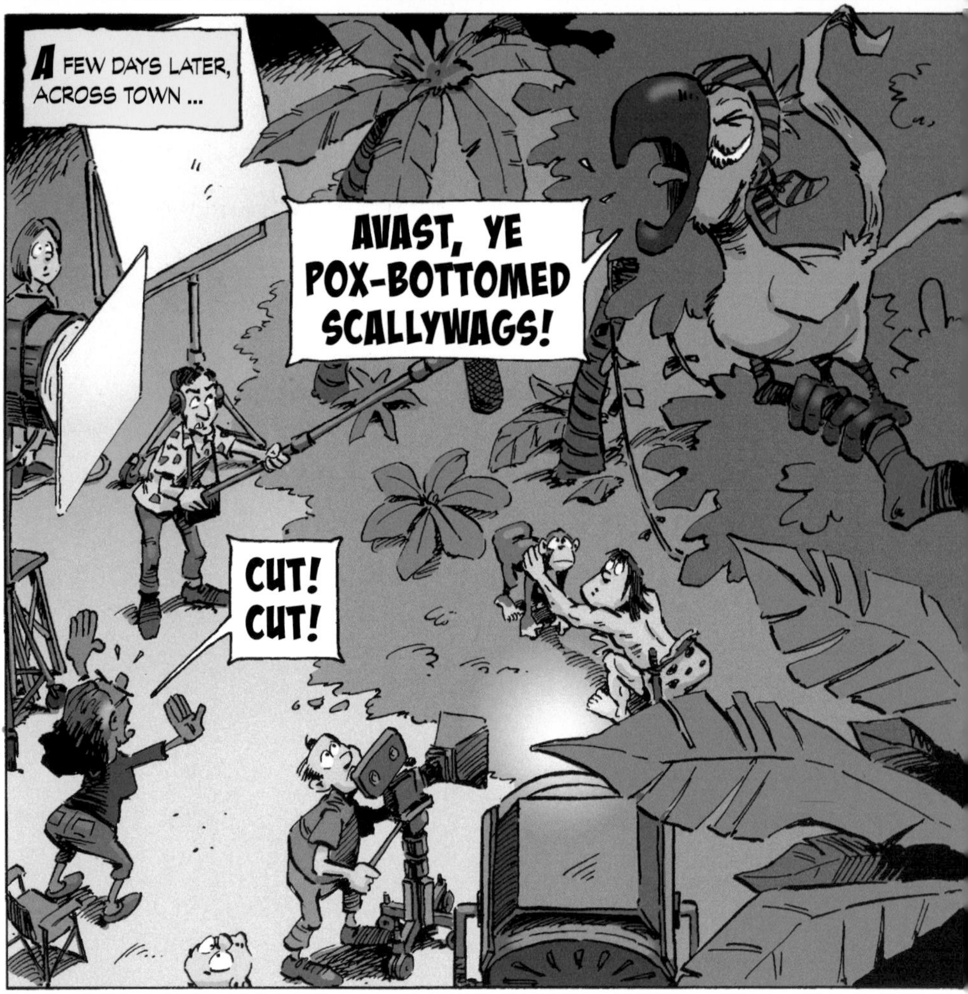
A FEW DAYS LATER, ACROSS TOWN ...
AVAST, YE POX-BOTTOMED SCALLYWAGS!
CUT! CUT!

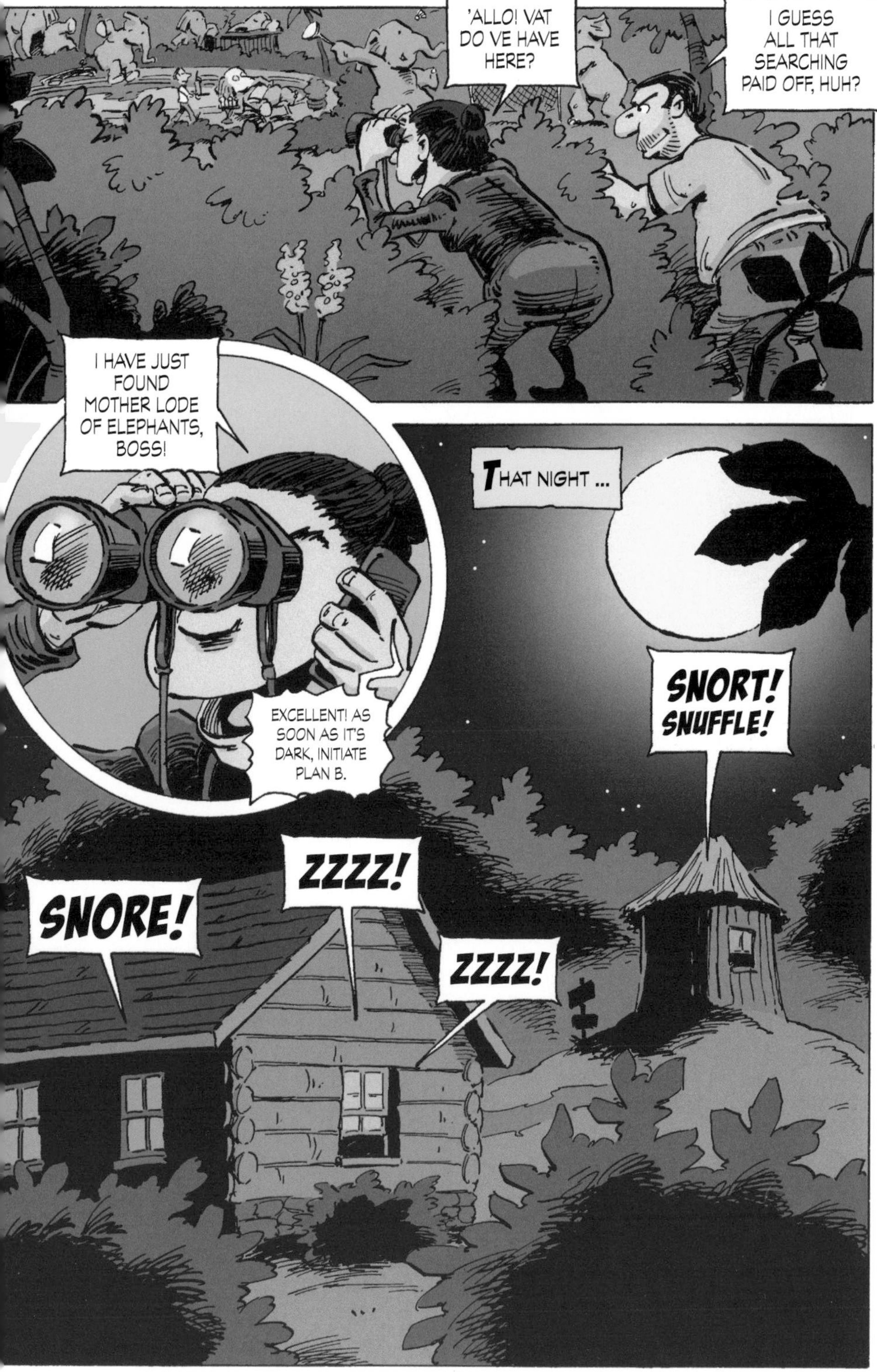
'ALLO! VAT DO VE HAVE HERE?
I GUESS ALL THAT SEARCHING PAID OFF, HUH?
I HAVE JUST FOUND MOTHER LODE OF ELEPHANTS, BOSS!
EXCELLENT! AS SOON AS IT'S DARK, INITIATE PLAN B.
THAT NIGHT ...
SNORT! SNUFFLE!
SNORE!
ZZZZ!
ZZZZ!

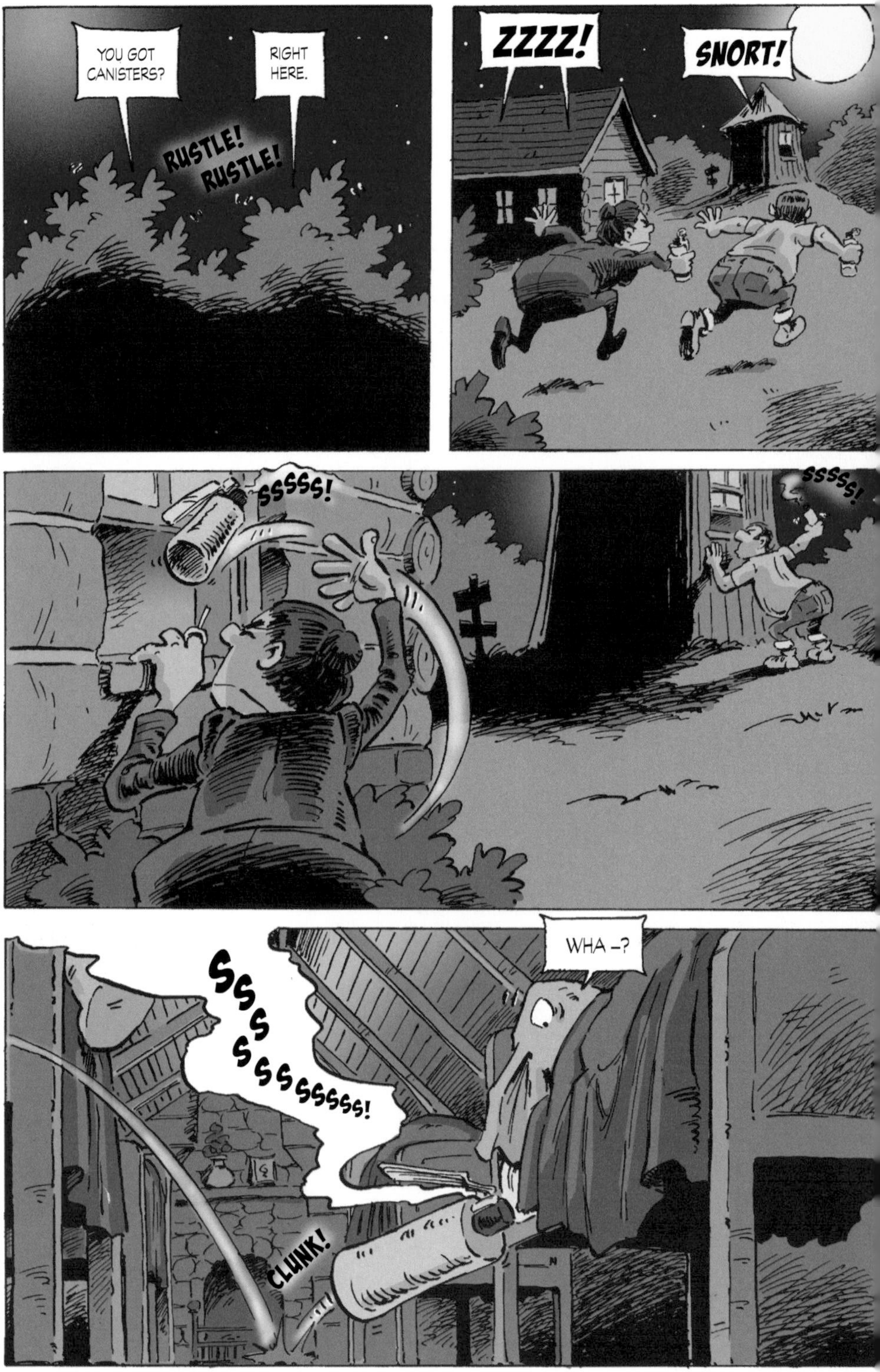
YOU GOT CANISTERS?
RIGHT HERE.
RUSTLE! RUSTLE!
ZZZZ!
SNORT!
SSSSS!
SSSSS!
WHA –?
SSSSSSSSSSS!
CLUNK!

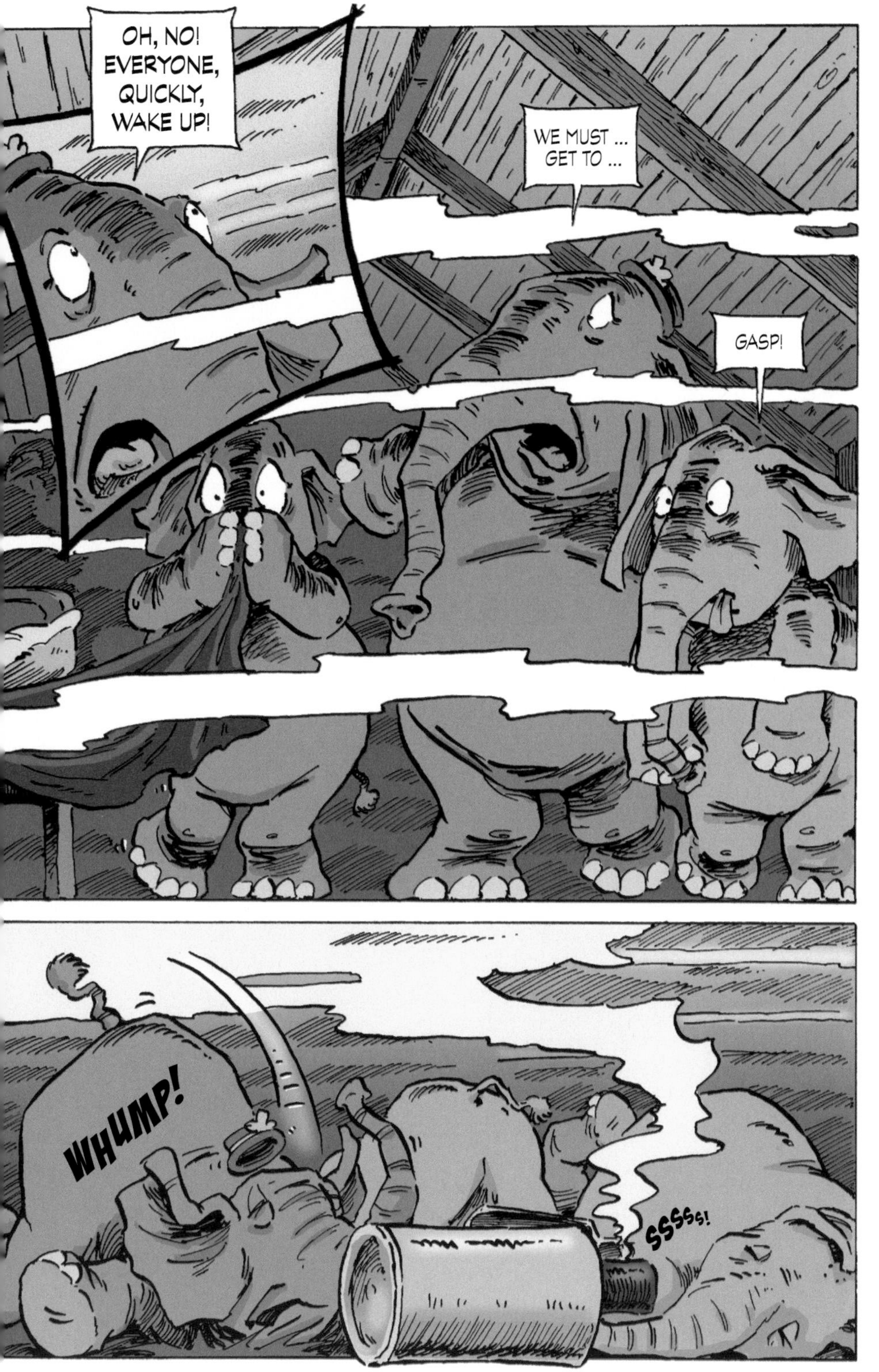
OH, NO! EVERYONE, QUICKLY, WAKE UP!
WE MUST ... GET TO ...
GASP!
WHUMP!
SSSSS!

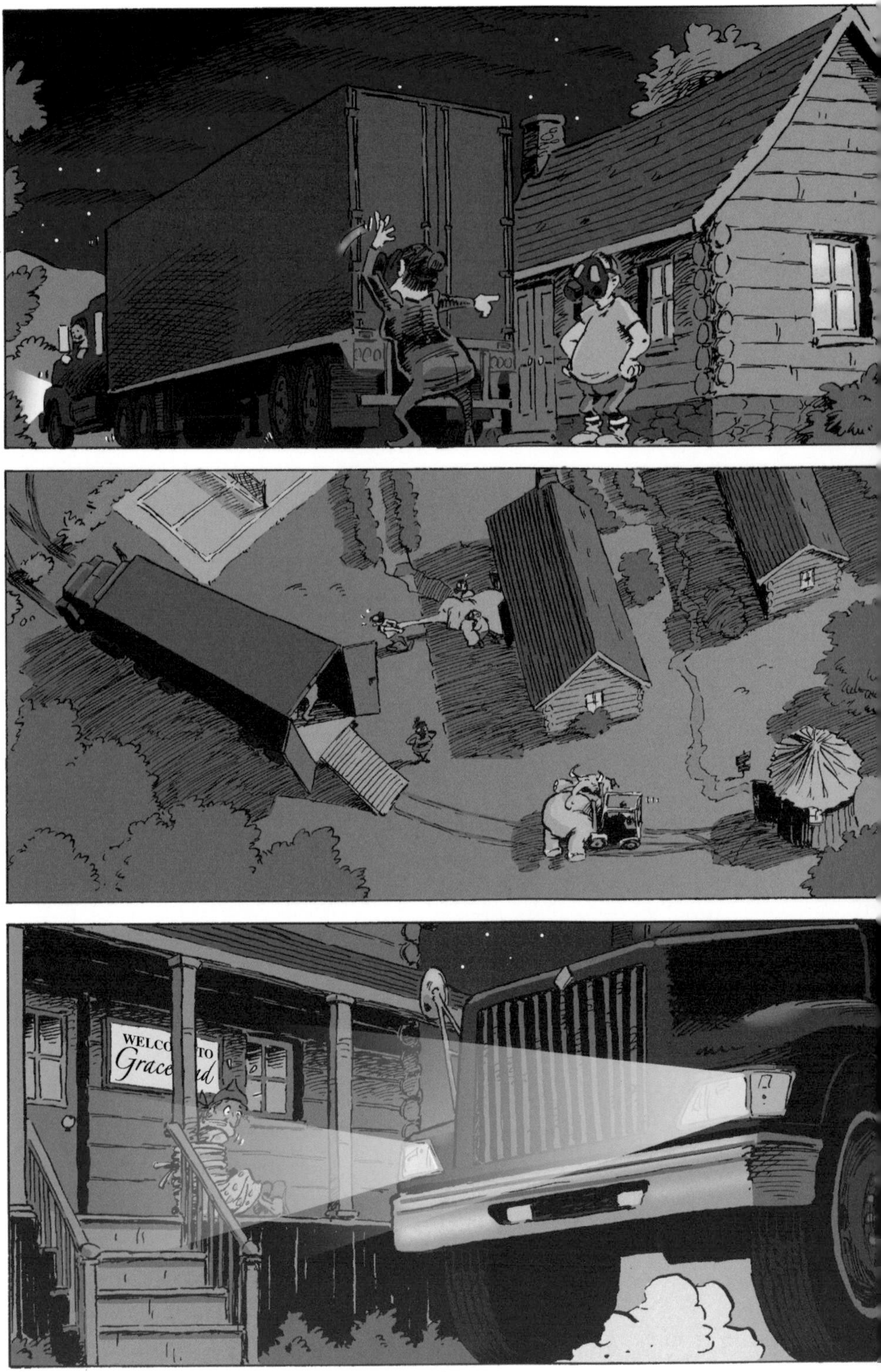
WELCO TO
Grace ad

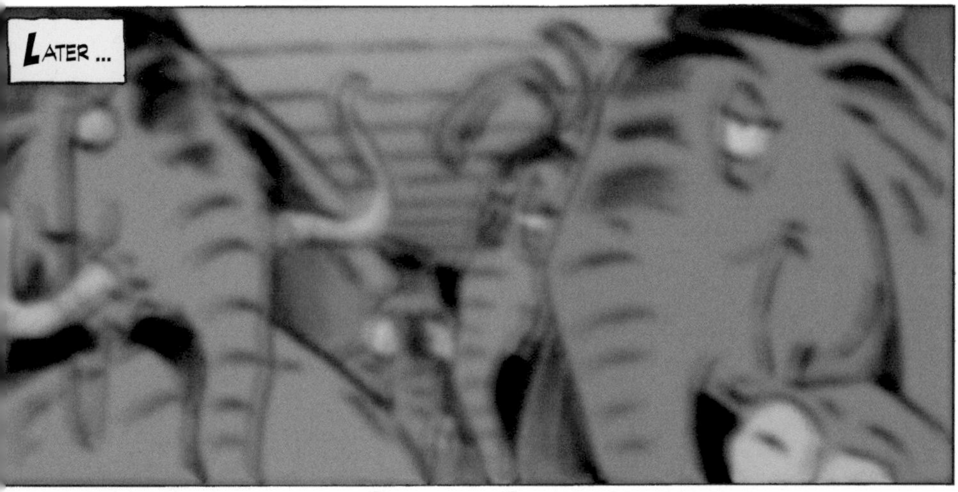
LATER ...

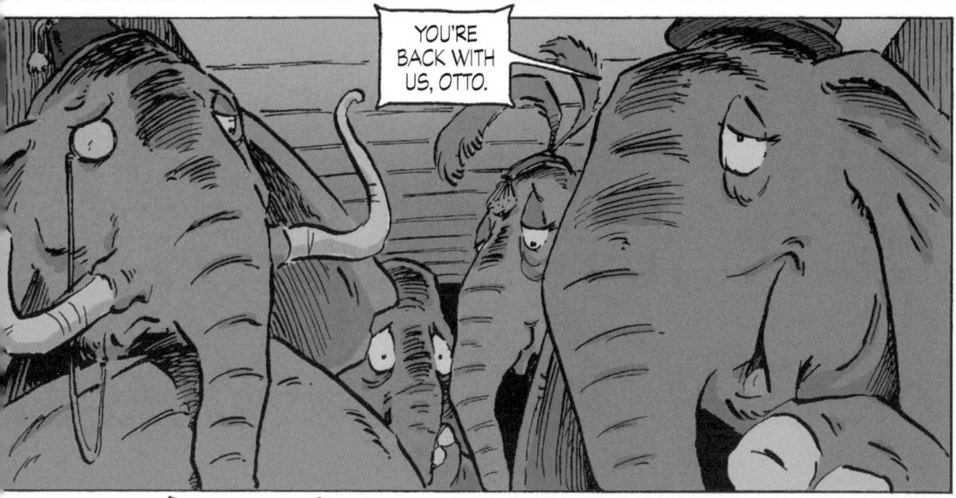
YOU'RE BACK WITH US, OTTO.

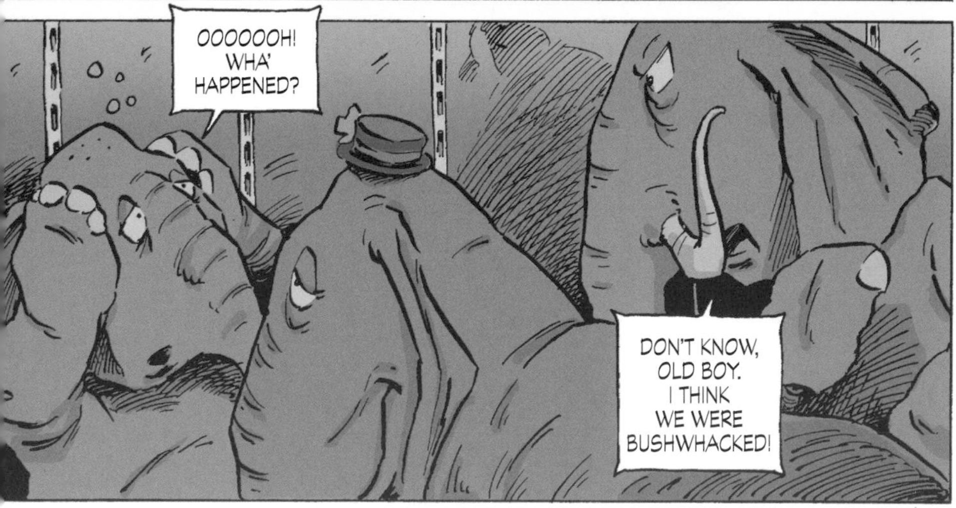
OOOOOOH! WHA' HAPPENED?
DON'T KNOW, OLD BOY. I THINK WE WERE BUSHWHACKED!

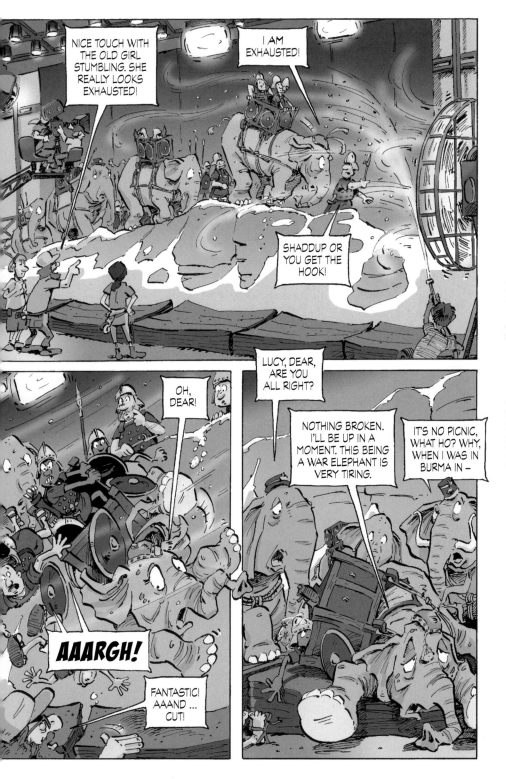

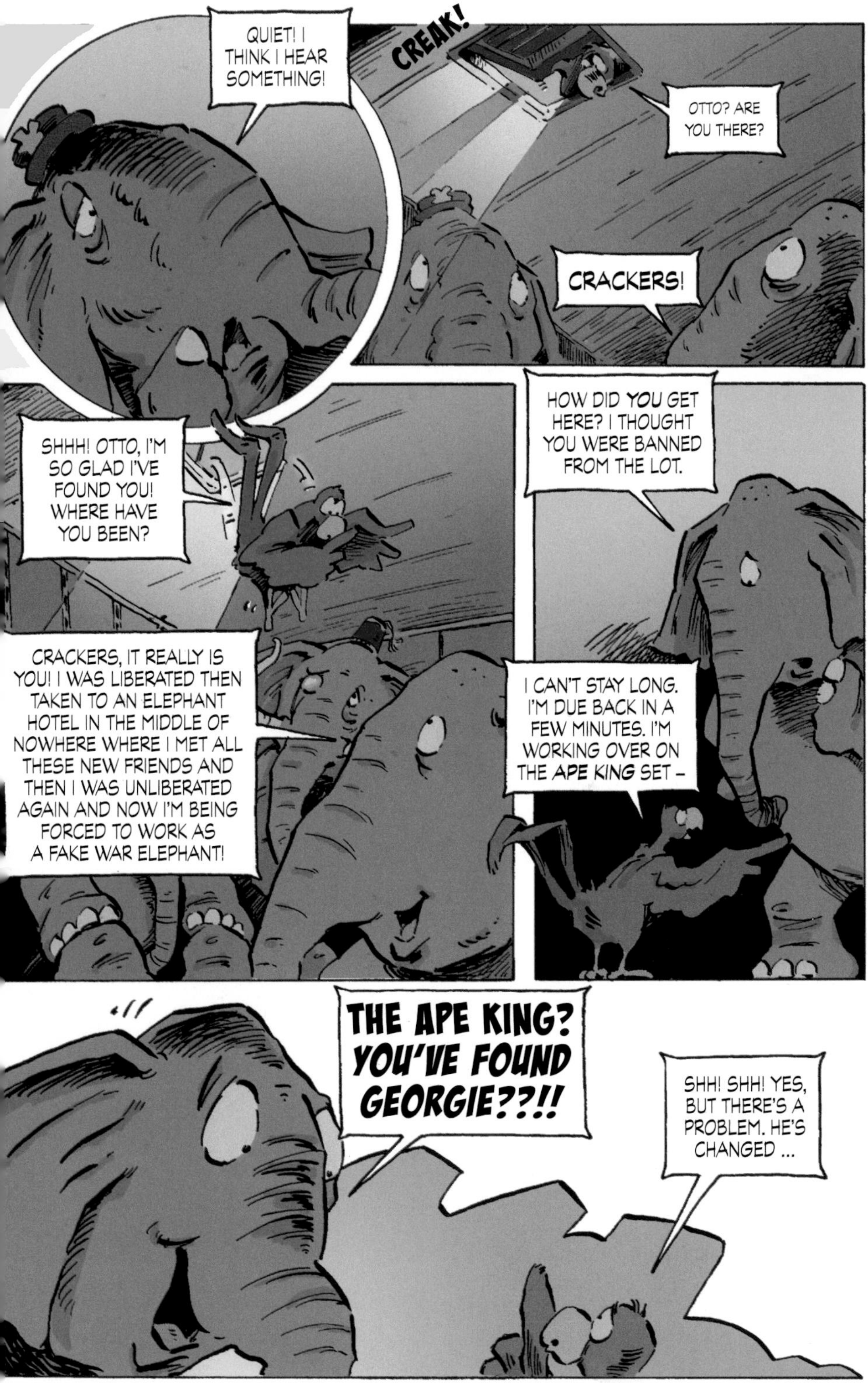
QUIET! I THINK I HEAR SOMETHING!
CREAK!
OTTO? ARE YOU THERE?
CRACKERS!
SHHH! OTTO, I'M SO GLAD I'VE FOUND YOU! WHERE HAVE YOU BEEN?
HOW DID YOU GET HERE? I THOUGHT YOU WERE BANNED FROM THE LOT.
CRACKERS, IT REALLY IS YOU! I WAS LIBERATED THEN TAKEN TO AN ELEPHANT HOTEL IN THE MIDDLE OF NOWHERE WHERE I MET ALL THESE NEW FRIENDS AND THEN I WAS UNLIBERATED AGAIN AND NOW I'M BEING FORCED TO WORK AS A FAKE WAR ELEPHANT!
I CAN'T STAY LONG. I'M DUE BACK IN A FEW MINUTES. I'M WORKING OVER ON THE APE KING SET –
THE APE KING? YOU'VE FOUND GEORGIE??!!
SHH! SHH! YES, BUT THERE'S A PROBLEM. HE'S CHANGED ...

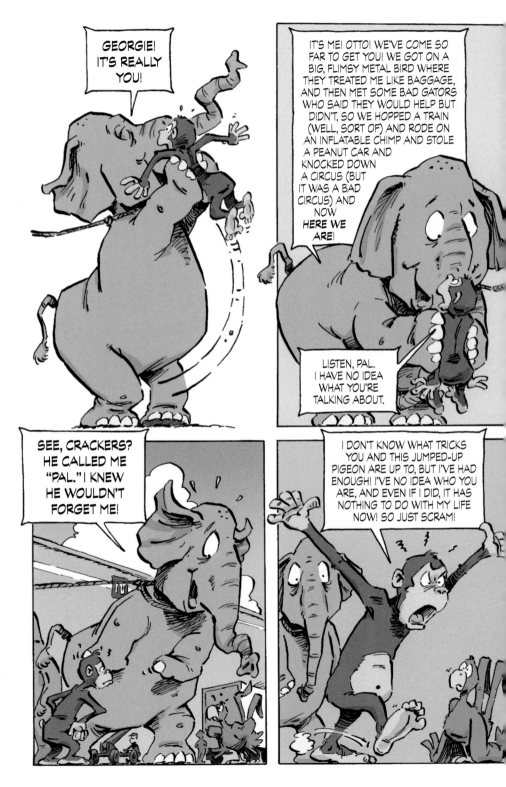

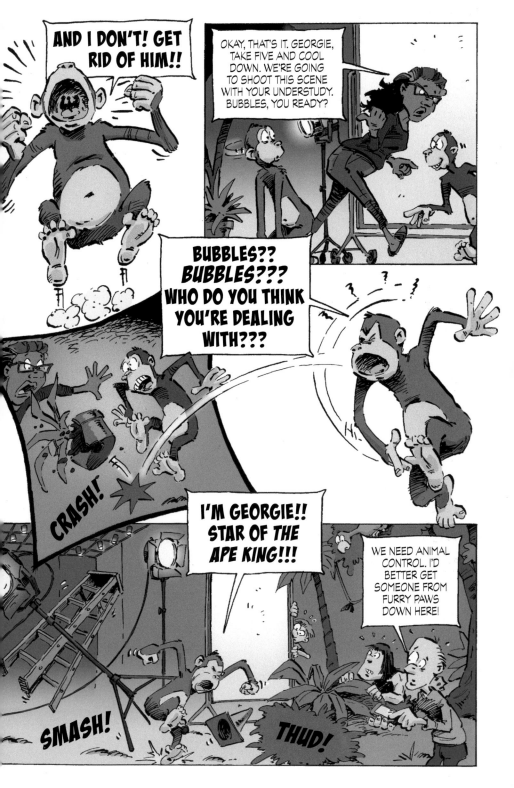

69

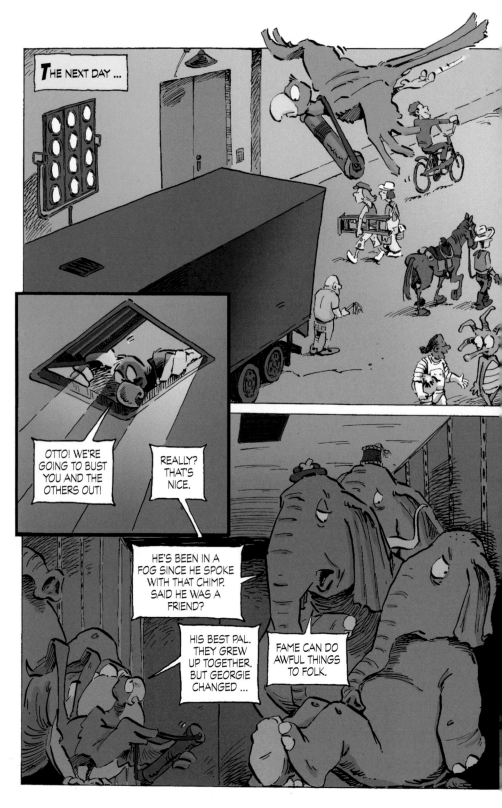

THE NEXT DAY ...

OTTO! WE'RE GOING TO BUST YOU AND THE OTHERS OUT!

REALLY? THAT'S NICE.

HE'S BEEN IN A FOG SINCE HE SPOKE WITH THAT CHIMP. SAID HE WAS A FRIEND?

HIS BEST PAL. THEY GREW UP TOGETHER. BUT GEORGIE CHANGED ...

FAME CAN DO AWFUL THINGS TO FOLK.

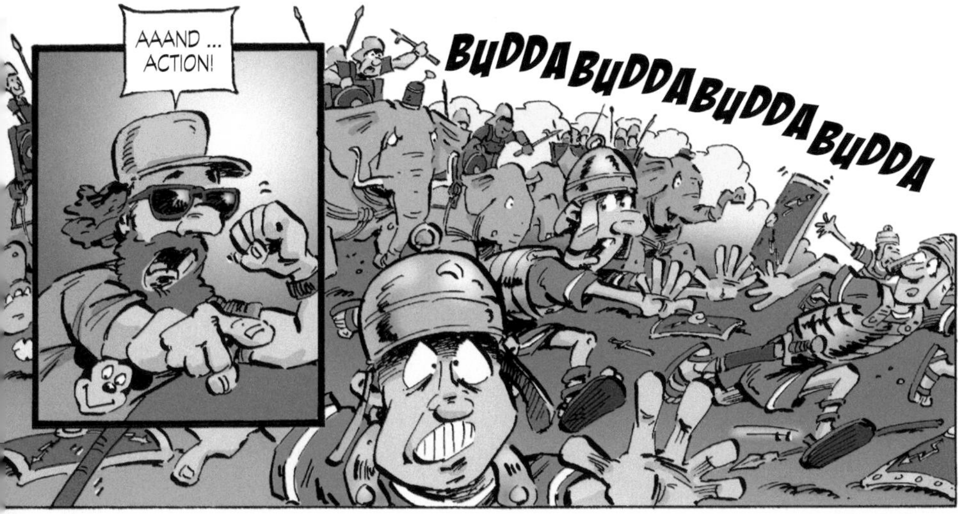
AAAND ... ACTION!
BUDDABUDDABUDDABUDDA

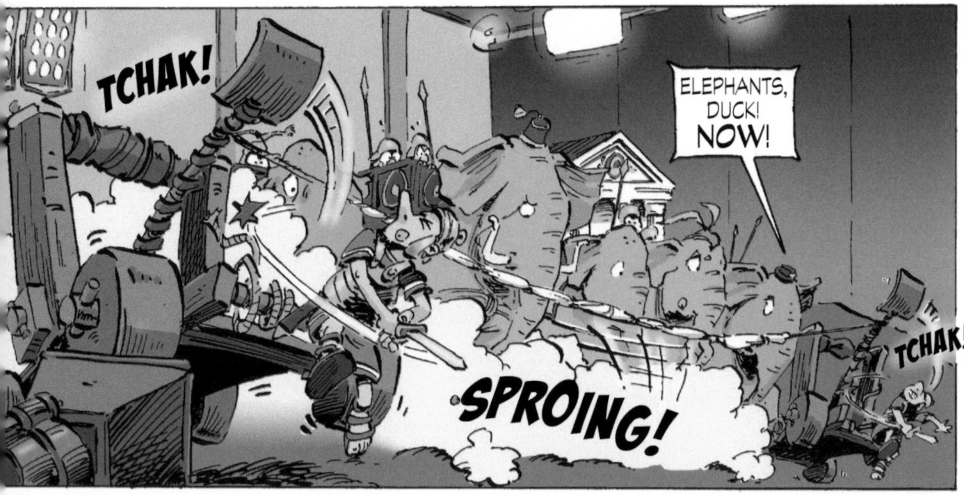
TCHAK!
ELEPHANTS, DUCK! NOW!
TCHAK!
SPROING!

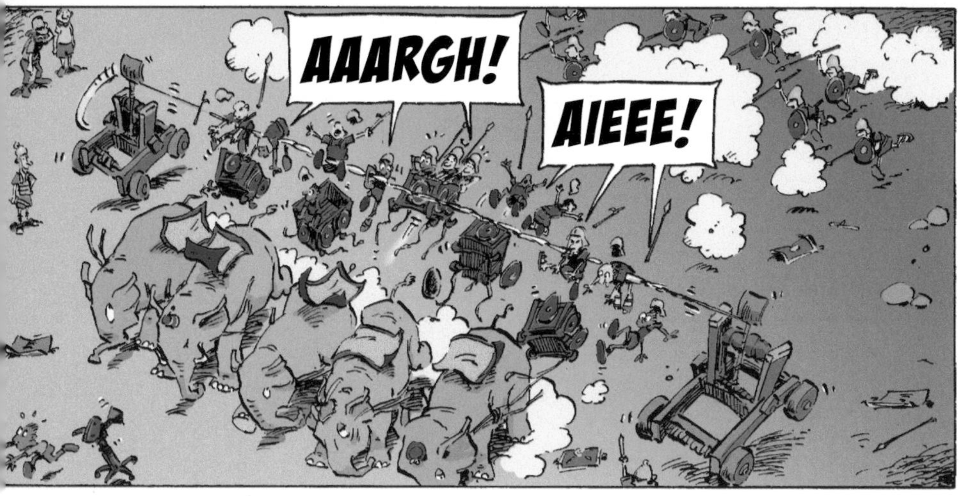
AAARGH!
AIEEE!

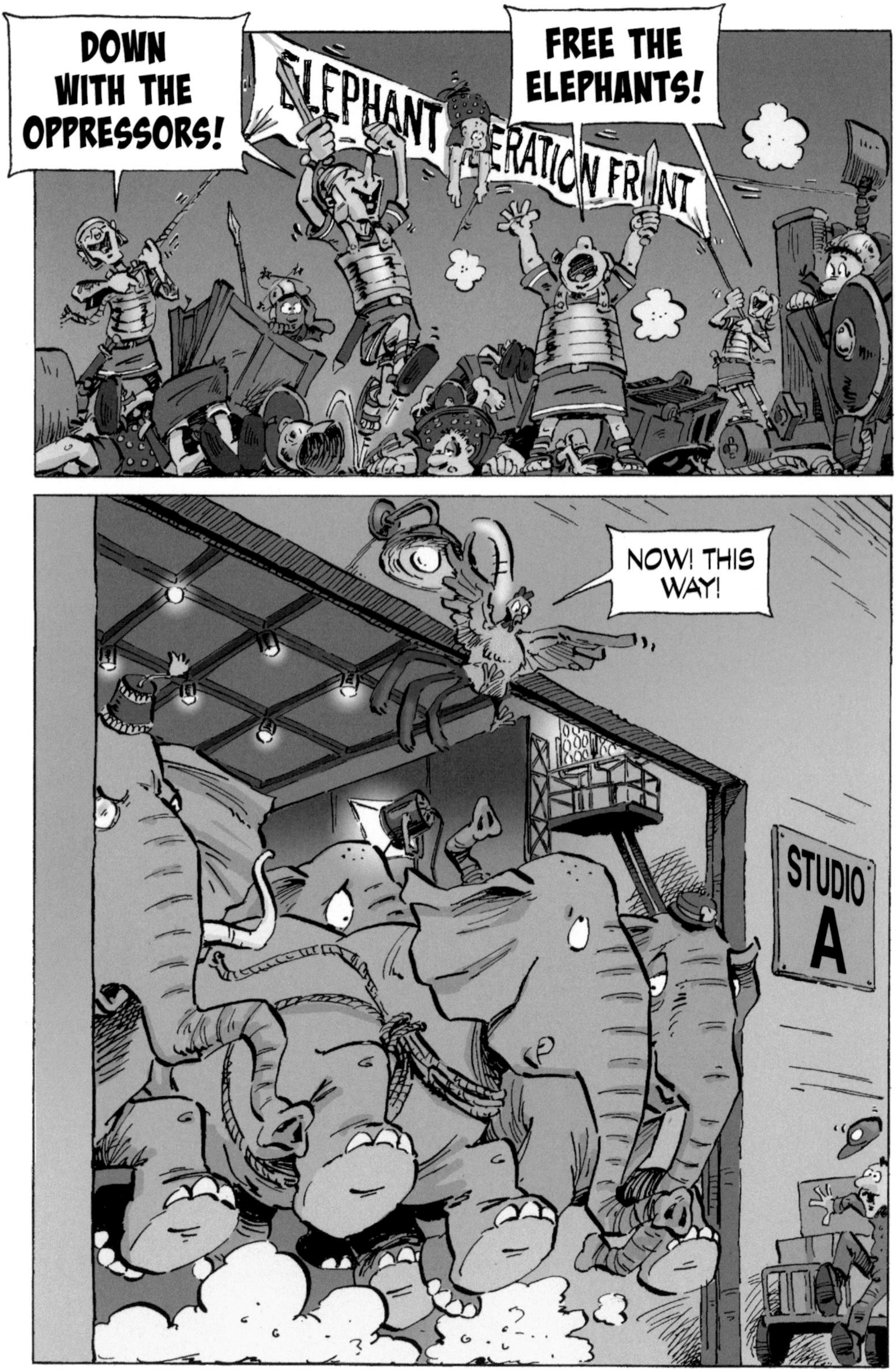
DOWN WITH THE OPPRESSORS!
FREE THE ELEPHANTS!
ELEPHANT
NOW! THIS WAY!
STUDIO A

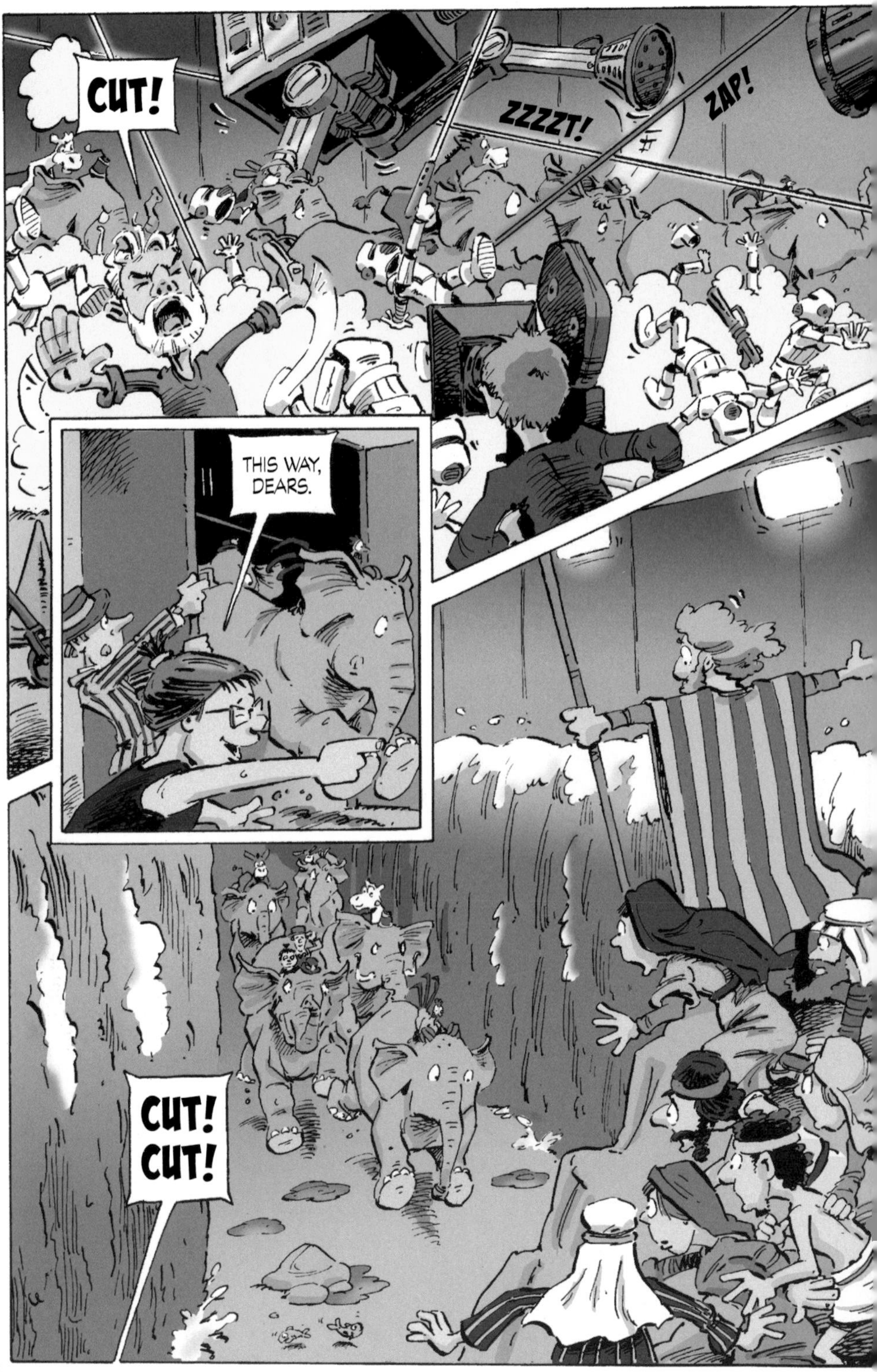
CUT!
ZZZZT!
ZAP!
THIS WAY, DEARS.
CUT! CUT!

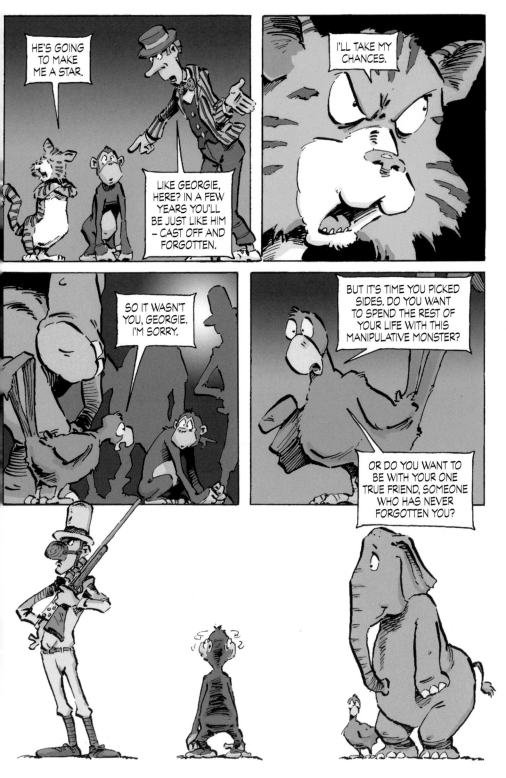

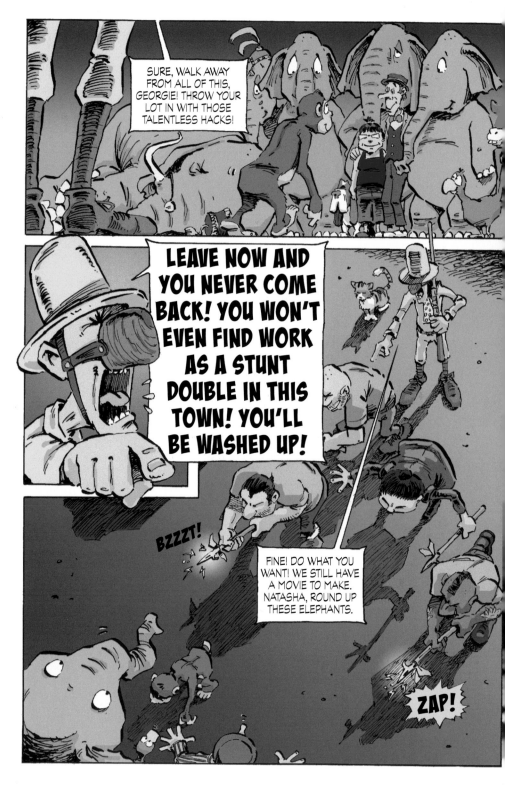

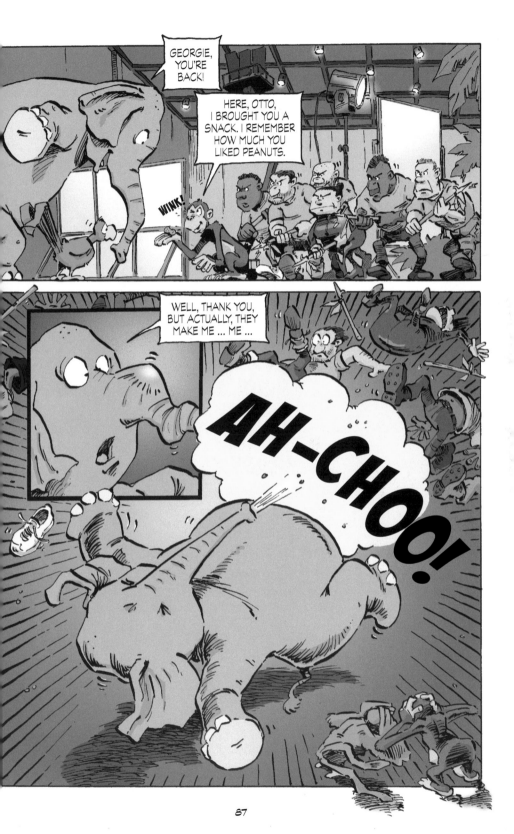

91

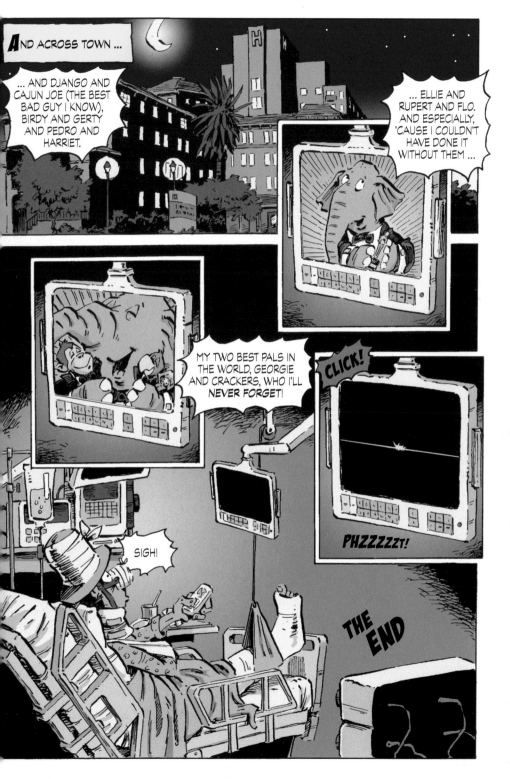

FOR ALBERTO UDERZO, WHO TAUGHT ME EVERYTHING I KNOW

Text © 2015 Bill Slavin with Esperança Melo
Illustrations © 2015 Bill Slavin

Kids Can Press acknowledges the financial support of the Government of Ontario, through the Ontario Media Development Corporation's Ontario Book Initiative; the Ontario Arts Council; the Canada Council for the Arts; and the Government of Canada, through the CBF, for our publishing activity.

Published in Canada by
Kids Can Press Ltd.
25 Dockside Drive
Toronto, ON M5A 0B5

Published in the U.S. by
Kids Can Press Ltd.
2250 Military Road
Tonawanda, NY 14150

www.kidscanpress.com

The artwork in this book was rendered in pen and ink line and colored in Photoshop.
The text is set in Graphite Std Narrow and BadaBoom Pro BB.

Edited by Stacey Roderick
Designed by Bill Slavin and Marie Bartholomew

The hardcover edition of this book is smyth sewn casebound.
The paperback edition of this book is limp sewn with a drawn-on cover.
Manufactured in Buji, Shenzhen, China, in 8/2014 by WKT Company

CM 15 0 9 8 7 6 5 4 3 2 1
CM PA 15 0 9 8 7 6 5 4 3 2 1

Library and Archives Canada Cataloguing in Publication

Slavin, Bill, author, illustrator
     Big star Otto / written by Bill Slavin with Esperança Melo;
art by Bill Slavin.

(Elephants never forget ; 3)
ISBN 978-1-894786-96-6 (bound)   ISBN 978-1-894786-97-3 (pbk.)

     1. Graphic novels. I. Melo, Esperança, author II. Title.
III. Series: Slavin, Bill. Elephants never forget ; 3.

PN6733.S55B527 2014   J741.5'971   C2014-903327-3

Kids Can Press is a CORUS™ Entertainment company